PENGUIN MODERN CLASSICS

If I Die Before I Wake

In writing *If I Die Before I Wake*, Sherwood King left a legacy of classic suspense writing, much copied and later immortalised in film.

SHERWOOD KING

If I Die Before I Wake

PENGUIN BOOKS

To Jacques Dun Lany

PENGUIN CLASSICS

Published by the Penguin Group
Penguin Books Ltd, 80 Strand, London WC2R 0RL, England
Penguin Group (USA) Inc., 375 Hudson Street, New York, New York 10014, USA
Penguin Group (Canada), 90 Eglinton Avenue East, Suite 700, Toronto, Ontario, Canada M4P 2Y3
(a division of Pearson Penguin Canada Inc.)
Penguin Ireland, 25 St Stephen's Green, Dublin 2, Ireland (a division of Penguin Books Ltd)
Penguin Group (Australia), 250 Camberwell Road, Camberwell, Victoria 3124, Australia
(a division of Pearson Australia Group Pty Ltd)
Penguin Books India Pvt Ltd, 11 Community Centre, Panchsheel Park, New Delhi – 110 017, India
Penguin Group (NZ), 67 Apollo Drive, Rosedale, North Shore 0632, New Zealand
(a division of Pearson New Zealand Ltd)
Penguin Books (South Africa) (Pty) Ltd, 24 Sturdee Avenue, Rosebank,
Johannesburg 2196, South Africa

Penguin Books Ltd, Registered Offices: 80 Strand, London WC2R 0RL, England

www.penguin.com

First published 1938
Published in Penguin Classics 2010
002

Set in Dante MT Std 10.5/13 pt
Typeset by Palimpsest Book Production Limited, Grangemouth, Stirlingshire
Printed in England by Clays Ltd, St Ives plc

978-0-141-19219-2

www.greenpenguin.co.uk

PART ONE

I

'Sure,' I said, 'I would commit murder. If I had to, of course, or if it was worth my while.'

I said this as though I meant it too. I didn't mean it. I didn't mean it at all.

'The way I figure it,' I said, 'a man's got to die some time. All murder does is hurry it up. What more is there to it?'

You know – talk. What any young fellow might say, just to show he's not afraid of anything.

There had been a murder out our way. On Long Island. Some society woman had shot her husband. He hadn't been doing anything, just raiding the icebox for a midnight snack. But (she said) she'd thought he was a burglar . . . five bullets' worth. Police were holding her; some insurance angle.

Anyway, that's what started Grisby talking about murder. I'd been driving him down to the railroad station every other day or so, whenever he'd come out to see my boss, Bannister, the lawyer. They were partners, only Bannister didn't get down to the office much. He had a twisted leg – something he'd got in the War. It made him walk funny . . . you could hardly get him outside, except to appear in court, and then only when he had to. But it didn't matter. He could work just as well at home, provided Grisby kept him in touch and came out often, and he did.

So this time driving down to the station we were talking about murder and Grisby asked me what I thought and I told him.

Afterwards I remembered he'd been building up to it from the very first. Nothing definite. Just letting me know one way and another that he thought I was too good to stay chauffeur to a man like Bannister for long. That he thought I was too smart not to have my eye on the main chance.

And there I was, taking it all in, trying to talk and act up to the role he'd given me and all the time not meaning a word of it, not a word.

It's like when a slick salesman gets hold of you. You don't want what he's selling, maybe, but you take it. You take it because you'd rather do that than let him think you weren't so smart after all.

Well, he liked it, too, my talking the way I did. He seemed to get a real kick out of it.

'I thought you were smart, Laurence,' he said. 'Now I know it.'

'Sure,' I said. 'All that silly sentimental stuff – if you want someone out of the way, why, get him out of the way.'

'But don't forget,' he said, 'you're smart only so long as you don't get caught. That's the difference between the smart man and the fool. The smart man doesn't get caught.'

'Oh, I didn't mean I really was going to kill anyone,' I said.

I stepped the car up to sixty to get some breeze and we rolled along without saying anything until we got to the station.

The station was empty as it usually was in the afternoons and there was no sign of the train.

Grisby got out and rested his briefcase on the running board, looking up at me as though he thought I was the goods, all right. I began to feel a little embarrassed.

'You'll be late for dinner,' I said.

He laughed.

'Dinner's a joke at my place, and I don't mind telling you that.'

He took off his panama and his glasses – pince nez, with a black ribbon – and began running a handkerchief over his face. The heat was bad enough for me, but it was worse for him. He weighed all of two hundred pounds – not fat, because he was as tall as I, and powerful, but it was plenty enough in that heat. Still, he was cheerful about it, as he always was, a real glad hander and hail fellow well met.

'How do you mean, a joke?' I asked.

'Wait till you get married, like I've been these last fifteen years. And the devil of it is, she won't give me a divorce.'

'Oh, I see. Not much you can do in a case like that, is there?'

He laughed again and fitted the glasses back on, looking up the railroad tracks. The train was coming, its whistle blowing.

'No,' he said, 'except maybe catch her raiding the icebox some night.'

I don't know whether it was the sound of the train whistle moaning over the swamp beside the tracks or something in the way Grisby talked, but all at once a shiver went up and down my spine.

'Sure,' I said, 'if it's the only way out, why not?'

He picked up his briefcase and looked at me, smiling.

'By God,' he said admiringly, 'I believe you would at that!'

Every once in a while after that he'd drop a hint or say something that would draw me out, always making me feel swelled up with my own importance, and all of a sudden it was too late for me to back down, and he had me.

II

It got to be then that the hardest thing I had to do was drive Grisby to the station.

Worst thing about it was that there wasn't anything definite. Something was coming up, something he was counting on me for. But that's all I knew. And I wouldn't ask him; I didn't want anything to do with it. I wasn't any angel, I'd been a sailor on tramps and knocked around a lot, but I wasn't *that* tough.

The thing to do, I figured, was bluff it out. Then, if it came right down to it, I'd blow. This job was all I'd been able to get ashore in over a year, and Bannister had been plenty good to me, but I wasn't getting mixed up in any murder – not me.

I cut out all the bragging and talked as little as possible. There was a strained feeling between us, but if he noticed it he never said anything. We'd talk about the weather or who was going to win the World Series – things like that.

Then, as though we'd both been thinking about it all the time but just hadn't been saying anything, he said, 'Well, Laurence, I've got it all figured out, and it's a beauty.'

'Swell,' I said. I was glad I had the wheel to handle and the road to watch.

'What do you say to five thousand dollars? Could you use it?'

'Could I!'

'I thought so . . . well, it's all settled, then. You'll have your money within a week.'

'Now I know you're kidding. Who's going to give me all that money, and for what?'

'Why, I'm going to give it to you. Right out of my own pocket.'

'I'll bet!'

It was funny, but all at once the strain between us was gone, and I swung the car in beside the station and cut the switch without feeling I needed to be holding the wheel any more. There was even a smile on my lips.

I said: 'Who is it you want murdered – your wife?'

He looked at me as though he didn't get it. Then he shook his head and laughed.

'You're a tough one, all right,' he said. He sank back. 'Have a cigarette?'

I took one out of a silver case he had. My hand didn't shake, if that's what he wanted to see.

'Well?' I asked. I put it right up to him. 'Who?'

We lighted up. Then he blew out smoke, saying:

'No, Laurence, the one you're going to kill is – me.'

'You!'

We looked at each other, his hard eyes bright with real amusement.

I said: 'You're not serious—'

'Certainly I am. I told you I'd figured it all out. It's got to be me. You know, they talk about the perfect crime. There's some defect in all of them. Ours will be the perfect crime, perfectly executed. And the first essential is that I be killed, the second that you be in a position to prove you killed me.'

'I can just see myself doing that!'

He laughed.

'Don't worry,' he said, 'you'll be anxious enough to prove it when the time comes. You just leave everything to me and do as I say and within a week you'll have your five thousand and everything will be fine.'

'Oh, then that was just a gag about me killing you? But that's what I said—'

'Sure it's what you said. And you know what I said, too – that I was serious. I am. You're going to fire a bullet into me and throw my body in the Sound. We'll have witnesses—'

'What the hell,' I said.

'That's just what the police will say, just what we want them to say, "what the hell!"'

'But I don't get it. What good is that going to do us, letting them know I killed you?'

'I thought you were smart.'

'Sure, but—'

'You're going to kill me, and yet you aren't. Now does it begin to make sense?'

'It's too deep for me.'

'Perfect!'

His yellow green eyes were telling me things, but I wasn't getting them. I was looking at the knot of his tie. It was a black one with yellow specks.

'Listen!' he said. 'They've got to produce a body, haven't they?'

I wasn't sure I liked all this. I kept looking at the tie. The yellow specks were tiny daggers.

'They've got to produce a body, and they can do all the shouting they want, but they can't do a single, blessed thing unless they can find the body. Isn't that right?'

'Yes, I guess it is.'

'And the body, Laurence, will be on a ship bound for the South Seas, where I've always wanted to go anyway. Now is it clear to you?'

I began to see a light.

'You want to cut loose from your wife, you mean, and you're taking this way of doing it?'

'Partly that – sure, say we put it that way. It will certainly do the trick, won't it?'

'But are you sure they can't do anything?'

'I'm a criminal lawyer, I ought to be sure, oughtn't I?'

'Yes, but—'

'But what?'

'Well, they might keep me in jail until the body turned up – and it never would. Not if you'd be cruising around down in the South Seas.'

He snorted.

'Suppose they did put you in jail for a while, or even in the psychopathic ward, if they thought you were nuts, what of it? Let 'em. Any dumb lawyer could get you out, if they didn't even have a body – and they won't have. I'll see to that. Besides, what's a little while in jail compared to five thousand waiting for you when you get out?'

'Yes, but—'

'Don't be a sap with all your "yes, buts." You get five thousand dollars for saying you killed me and proving it. And you're absolutely safe. You haven't a thing to worry about.'

'But supposing they find you? You've got insurance, haven't you? The insurance people will want to be certain you're dead. They may check the steamship companies. It might not be as easy as it looks.'

'You just leave everything to me. I'll be dead, all right. They won't pay the insurance without a death certificate, but it doesn't matter, either. My wife's got money in her own name – enough to keep her the rest of her life. So don't let the insurance part of it worry you. How about it, is it a deal?'

I took a deep draw on my cigarette.

'I'll think it over,' I said.

His eyebrows shot up.

'You mean you want to think over whether you could use that five thousand?'

'Oh, I could use that, all right.'

'You just don't know how you'd spend it – that's what's worrying you? You want to think it over?'

'I don't want to rush into anything, that's all.'

He slapped me on the knee.

'Perfect!' he said. 'That's just the way I'd hoped you'd be. It's what I mean about your being smart. Why, I wouldn't even put it past you if you'd already decided. Now what do you think about that?'

'I don't know. What do you think?'

'There you go again, answering a question with a question. That's another sure sign. But about thinking it over – of course you should. Why, do you know what I do when a client asks me a question or wants my advice? I might even have the answer on the tip of my tongue – but do I give it? Oh, no. I wait for the ball to bounce. I walk up and down the room. I look out the window. If there's a pretty girl down on the street, I take just that much longer to reach a decision. Then when I give it, it carries some weight. It's worth more. But I don't need to tell you all these things. You know all the angles already.'

Sure I felt good – who wouldn't?

'Tell you the truth,' Grisby went on, 'if you hadn't said you'd think it over, you might never have heard another thing about it. I distrust a man who is too quick to reach decisions. You go right ahead and think it over. Take your time.'

He looked at his watch as though he were going to time me from that minute.

'The train isn't due for three and a half minutes,' he said. 'Tell me: you've been down in the South Seas, haven't you?'

'Sure – just about every other place, too. Why?'

'I'm just wondering where's the best place to go. How about Tahiti? Is it really all they say it is?'

'You go down there and you'll never want to leave. It's got everything.'

'You've certainly been around, haven't you? A man of the world, eh?'

'I don't know about that. I went on tramp steamers, first as an ordinary seaman and then as an A.B. But I'll tell you one thing – you sure learn a lot more that way than going around as a passenger on one of those ritzy liners. When you're on a tramp steamer, you go to all sorts of out-of-the-way places where the liners never stop, and you're treated like a king. I used to dress up at a port and go ashore to the best hotel and never go back to the ship until it was ready to sail. They'd dock me two days' pay for every day I stayed ashore, but what the hell – you might never get there again, so what of it? I'd get invited to all the best places, just because I was young and an American, and because most of the people from the States were bored to death living away from their friends. They'd want me to stay and load me down with gifts when I left – the girls particularly. You know, daughters of army officers and men down from the States on business.'

'How come you didn't marry any of them?'

'Oh, I could have, all right.'

'Some of them with money, too, I'll bet.'

'That's right. I just didn't want to get my money that way.'

'Well, it's just as easy to fall in love with a girl with money as one without – a lot easier, I'd say.'

'Maybe so. I just wasn't interested.'

'I should think they wouldn't have let you go, a good-looking fellow like you, and smart, too. But I suppose you weren't ready to settle down – you wanted to see the whole world first, eh?'

'I guess so.'

'No family waiting for their wandering boy to come home?'

'No. I never knew my parents. I lived on my uncle's farm in North Dakota. When he died I went to sea. I still have the farm, but the land's all shot up there and I can't even sell it. I'd always wanted to go to sea, but I never meant to make it my life. Not that I haven't done other things ashore, but none of them lasted very long, for one reason or another.'

'How'd you ever get with Bannister?'

'That just happened. It was getting harder and harder to get on a ship and I was pretty tired of it, anyway. I wanted to do things, amount to something. But I couldn't get a job on land, either. You know how things were. Finally I drifted out here on Long Island, thinking this is where all the rich people were and that I might get a job here. I was out here swimming when Bannister saw me.'

'He saw you come out of the water?'

'Yes. I came up on his beach. He called to me. He didn't mind me using his beach, but he was lying there in the sand and asked me about myself and I told him. Then he gave me the job. That's all.'

'Yes, I know,' Grisby said. 'But it's not why he hired you – just because he needed someone, I mean.'

'No?'

'No. He could have got dozens from the city, just by raising a finger.

He took you because you were young and good-looking and had such a marvelous physique.'

'That's silly,' I said. 'What difference would that make?'

He laughed.

'Just all the difference in the world,' he said. 'You mean he's never told you about his leg? It was in the War that it happened. This was before he was in the intelligence service. He was a lieutenant and was having a mess kitchen drawn up. A shell struck it. When he woke up in the hospital they told him his leg would have to come off.'

He waited so long I asked, 'Well, did they take it off?'

'No, they didn't. He wouldn't let them amputate. Said he'd rather die if that's the way it was. They did what they could, and managed to save his life, but the leg was twisted all out of shape and never could heal right. It made him bitter and a little screwy.'

'How do you mean – screwy?'

'Oh, he's got a quirk in his brain about youth shuffling along. Says they're wasting the most precious moments of life and don't know it. Thinks they ought to be doing something – you know, grasping the fruits while they're offered. All that rot. It's his idea that they might be crippled in the next hour themselves, like he is – how do they know they won't be? – and then the fruits would be denied them like they are him. Screwy? He's absolutely batty when he gets on the subject!'

'He's never said anything to me.'

'Well, he will, he will! He's been pretty busy, that's all. But it's why he hired you, you can bet on that. He likes to have people around who are young and straight, the way he'd like to be himself, so he can see them doing all the things he'd like to do, but can't because of his leg.'

'But he doesn't seem to be denied anything,' I said. 'He's got plenty of money, a swell big house, a beautiful young wife—'

'Yes, a beautiful young wife who hates him, who married him when she was eighteen, before she knew what it was all about, and has regretted it ever since.'

'Is that so? They seem to get along pretty well to me.'

'Why, figure it out! What would a girl like that, who's no older than you are, have in common with a man like Bannister? Always brooding about his bum leg. He's all washed up and doesn't know it.'

The train whistle sounded eerily along the swamp.

'Well, you think over our proposition,' he said, getting out.

III

I kept turning it over and over in my mind like a hot pancake.

Five thousand dollars!

That was a hell of a lot of dough. Not too much for getting myself in a jam on a murder rap, even if it was all set for me to go free. Something might always happen.

But it *was* too much for Grisby to pay just to make it look like he was dead. There'd have to be a better reason than wanting to leave his wife. If that was all there was to it, he could just pick up and go.

Another thing: the police would want to know why I'd killed him. They'd sweat it out of me. What could I tell them – robbery? They'd grab the five thousand, sure as shooting. What else? I checked them off, all the motives I could think of:

—Hate?

—Anger?

—Jealousy?

—Revenge?

It couldn't be any, as far as I could see. Robbery, yes. But that was out; it *had* to be out. Yet what other reason could there be for his partner's chauffeur to murder him and throw his body in the Sound?

Well, that was Grisby's problem, not mine. Only I wasn't rushing into the thing blindly. I'd have to know plenty first. Right now it looked fishy – fishy as hell.

Still – five thousand dollars! What I couldn't do with that! I thought of all the things I could do, sitting up in my room that night.

The room was over the garage. Mrs Bannister had done a swell job fixing it up. Bright drapes on the windows. A good clean bed. Bookshelves. A writing desk. A fireplace that would be great in the winter. All mine! The job was pretty soft, too. But the whole layout couldn't compare with five thousand dollars.

The phone rang. It was about nine o'clock. Mrs Bannister's husky low voice. Would I bring the car around? They were going down to the beach.

Bannister came out first, walking in that comic, jerky way his leg made him walk. He was wearing a long white robe with a cowl hanging loose and looked very handsome with his sleek black hair. Close up his features were too sharp, his cheeks too pinched for him to be really good-looking. Deep-set black eyes under dark brows gave him a brooding and defiant look.

'Good evening,' I said. 'Nice night for a swim.'

'Yes, isn't it?' His voice was cold.

I kicked myself, remembering he couldn't swim.

He had a blanket and towels and put them in the back of the car while I switched on the light.

'Where's your suit?' he asked.

'My suit?'

'Didn't you bring it?'

'Why, no. I—'

'Oh, you needn't stand on ceremony here. Glad to have you. If it's hot for us, it's hot for you, too. Besides, Mrs Bannister always swims out too far. That's dangerous at night. You can keep an eye on her. But hurry it up. On the run!'

I went up and grabbed the suit. When I came down again Mrs Bannister was there. She was standing beside the car in the light from the house. Just to look at her took my breath away. She had on a one-piece white suit without any back and her dark red hair hung loose and wild.

There was a bathhouse on the beach. I put on the trunks and came out and sat in the sand near Bannister. He was hunched up on the blanket smoking his pipe. I looked around for Mrs Bannister. She wasn't there.

The moon was up over the water and as far up and down the beach as you could see were little fires. Down a way a man was playing a guitar and a girl was singing.

We sat and listened. After a while a speedboat shot past in the water ahead of us and started cutting capers in the moonlight. It leaped and splashed over the water, its motor making a racket as the throttle was pushed to top speed.

Suddenly it cut in toward shore and charged straight for the landing on Bannister's beach.

Bannister started to jump up, then sank back as the motor was cut and the boat slid in to a stop.

Mrs Bannister jumped out, laughing and waving at Bannister.

Bannister bit his lip. She'd given him a scare – on purpose, it looked like.

'Better come in,' he called. 'We'll build a fire.'

She shook her head, ran up onto the diving board and dove in.

Bannister sighed.

'The water looks fine,' he said.

I looked at him; he was taking me in.

'Man, but you've got a build,' he said.

What could I say?

'It just looks that way,' I told him. 'A sailor not half my size beat the tar out of me once.'

'That's right, you were a sailor, weren't you?'

'Most of the time. I did other things, too. Sold house-to-house, drove a truck, worked on a newspaper—'

'You did!'

'Sure.'

I told him how I'd read every good book I could get my hands on while at sea, and how I'd been trying to write ever since a kid, even though I'd never got past the eighth grade out there at Goodrich, North Dakota.

'I thought I was getting somewhere when I got into newspaper work,' I said, 'and I even started going to City College nights. But when times got tough I found out, like a lot of other people, that my hands could get me three squares a day a lot better than my head could. So after I got laid off the paper, I got one of those real man-killing jobs driving a ten-ton truck around the country eighteen hours a day. That didn't last, either, so I dug out the old A.B. ticket again and went back to sea.'

He wasn't listening. He was watching his wife's arms going up and down in the path cut by the moonlight.

'Better go out and watch her,' he said.

His voice said a lot more than that. It said that she was precious to him . . . that he couldn't have anything happening to her.

I went out on the long pier and dove in.

It was deep here – a good place to say I'd dumped Grisby. I'd heard, too, that few bodies were ever recovered from the Sound. There was something about it that kept the body down, or carried it out to sea. That would work in good – if I went through with it.

The water was cold at first, but by the time I'd reached her it was fine.

She turned her head, smiling, and went right on. It was easy to keep up with her. Then she started to race me. The way she was going, I got the idea she didn't want me watching her, that she'd just as soon drown as not. I let her get ahead a little way and when she tired I came up fresh. She turned on her back and floated.

'The sky!' she said.

It seemed to be tumbling down on us a million miles a minute. You could almost hear it roar.

I kept still and watched. She hadn't been talking to me, I knew, but to herself.

Going back, she cut over toward a raft that was rolling in the water about fifty feet off shore. We held on to it out of breath, gasping. It had been a good swim.

'Help me up, please.'

I climbed onto the raft and reached down for her. She put one hand on my wrist and the other on my shoulder and came up easily, laughing. At the top she slipped and held on close. A shiver went through her. I put my hand on her back to steady her and felt her hair like dark seaweed in my face. My heart started pounding.

The raft bobbed in the water with a crazy motion, throwing us still closer. Her body pressed.

I looked over toward the beach. The fires were like fireflies. I couldn't see Bannister, everything looked blurred. I wondered if he could see us, in case anything happened.

Then the raft steadied and she sank down putting her hands behind her head, lying looking at the stars.

I felt pretty shaky. I had seen her now really for the first time not as a married woman I drove the car for but as someone very beautiful and near my own age.

I sat down next to her on the edge of the raft and tried to catch my breath in earnest now.

She was so near I could have leaned over and kissed her. I didn't. It would have to be her doing. I wasn't taking any chances losing my job.

After a while she raised herself on one elbow, looking at me and then up at the stars again.

'You can get me that big red one,' she said.

I didn't know what she meant. Then I saw it, too late. Mars. I guess she thought I was pretty dense.

She smiled and settled back.

'Hadn't you better go in and build a fire?' she asked.

Class dismissed.

I dove in and swam back slowly. I had a lot of thinking to do.

IV

Bannister was still puffing away on his pipe, the robe over his knees. He was wearing a blue and white striped jersey and looked very thin.

I said: 'Mrs Bannister would like a towel and her comb.'

'Oh, yes.'

'And her cigarettes.'

He fished them out of her bag, hesitating a little.

'Did she say she intended to stay out there? Tell her I'd rather she came in, won't you? We'll build a little fire. How was the water?'

I didn't want him to think he'd missed anything.

'A little too cold,' I said. 'I'll tell her.'

Now maybe there'd be a different story. At least, I'd give it another try. But I still wasn't going to start it myself.

She said: 'Oh, thank you. That was nice of you to think to bring my things.'

'Mr Bannister said—'

'Yes, I know. It's always the same. Tell him when I finish this cigarette. I want to lie here and watch the sky awhile. It's so glorious tonight.'

She began drying herself with the towel, humming the song they were playing down the beach. She didn't pay any more attention to me.

I left her on the raft and went back and found some wood and built a fire. I felt pretty small. Of course she wouldn't have anything to do with her chauffeur. She wasn't that sort.

We sat and watched the fire, Bannister scowling over his pipe and not saying a word. Now and then a couple would go past on the way from one party to another. They all seemed to fit in with the music; we didn't.

Suddenly a girl came running. She stumbled in the sand and got up laughing, looking over her shoulder. She had on a suit with a brassiere top tied in the back and her lips were very red in a brown face. A nice looking young fellow my age was right behind. He caught up to her in front of us and brought her to the sand with a shout. The laughing stopped. Her arms went around him and they lay still. After a while he lifted her up and carried her down the beach. Neither had even looked at us.

Bannister took out his pipe and stared at me.

'Good God, man,' he said, huskily. 'How can you sit there and not want to be a part of all that? How old are you?'

'Twenty-six.'

'Do you know how old I am?'

'Why, I'd say about – about forty.' I wished I'd said thirty-five.

'Well, I'm forty-three. Forty-three! Do you know what I'd give to be twenty-six again, with a build like yours?'

I said: 'You don't look forty-three.'

He laughed far down in his throat.

'No, but at forty-three how heavily my thousands of years of nothingness weigh upon me.'

I guessed it must be the night and the singing and the waves going up the shore. I smelled whiskey, though, and remembered he was strong for his Scotch and soda. Why, at his age he was still a young man. I wasn't too young to know that; I'd seen sailors tough as marlinspikes at sixty and seventy even, but then, there was that leg of his. That was really what was behind it, probably.

'And the pity of it is,' he said, 'when you're young you can't imagine yourself being old and wanting the chance to be young again. If you could, you would regulate everything differently, I assure you. Wasn't it Voltaire who suggested that we make love in our youth, and in old age attend to salvation?'

What did he think, I should be out making love? That was a good one.

'There's a poem I like to recite,' he said. 'Would you care to hear it?'

'Sure.' I was getting paid for it.

'It goes like this.' He leaned forward, his face at once dark and bright in the firelight, his voice at once eager and old:

'A Moment's Halt – a momentary taste
Of Being from the Well amid the Waste—
And Lo! – the phantom Caravan has reach'd
The Nothing it set out from – Oh, make haste!'

'That's swell,' I said.

He looked at me with the left eyebrow raised for a minute, and then shrugged. I thought he was going to drop the whole thing and give me up as a total loss. I started to poke the fire and go look for more wood, but he stopped me.

'Listen!' he snapped.

He was tighter than I'd thought. Then I spotted the bottle on the blanket and knew he'd been hitting it all the time we were out swimming. I sat down and let him talk, without listening very hard . . . all about the things that were denied him because of his leg, so he couldn't 'make haste' if he wanted to. But what made him boil most was that those who *could* weren't doing anything about it, like me. They were asleep and maybe never would wake up. Maybe never until they were about to die. And then it was too late to wake.

What the hell, I thought.

'Myself, in the War . . . going on leave, knowing that the next moment might be the last – seeing how cheap life could be, even my own—'

Mrs Bannister, coming into the firelight suddenly, gave me a scare. I guessed she'd been listening.

'Marco, for heaven's sake,' she said. 'Again?'

'Yes, Elsa,' he mimicked her. 'Again!'

She seemed surprised and not quite sure that she had heard right.

'Don't you ever get tired of the same—' She stopped, looking at him with her lips still parted.

His eyes blazed yellow in the firelight. Veins stood out on his neck and forehead. If I hadn't known he'd been drinking, I'd have been surprised, too.

'I get tired of the attitude you adopt, that I am a child to be humored—'

She hadn't been trying to humor him, just to be nice.

'Oh, it isn't that; you know it isn't. It's only—'

'What? Only what? We might as well face this thing, Elsa, now as any other time. I needn't tell you how strangely you've been acting lately. I think I have the right—'

For a minute they just stared at each other, Mrs Bannister getting more and more burned up each second.

I guessed the fuse had been burning quite a while, that they'd been over and over this time and again before and were only taking the argument up where they'd left off.

And there I was, watching the whole thing like a play. I wanted to get up and leave, but couldn't.

'You!' she said. Her lips twitched. 'Always thinking of yourself! What about me – what about *my* youth?'

She was dripping wet and the white suit clung to her and her smooth brown skin glistened with drops of water. There didn't seem to be anything the matter with *her* youth. Anger just made her more beautiful.

With neither of them paying any attention to me, I took her all in . . . the full, pointed breasts, quivering now with her breathing; the slim brown legs and smooth bare back and shoulders; the small straight nose, brown eyes and large red lips, that made me want to crush them – hard.

'Your youth!' said Bannister. 'If it hadn't been for me, you'd still be wasting your youth in the chorus, three shows a day until you dropped. And before that, what were you? Nothing – you didn't have a cent.'

So that was it – she'd been a chorus girl. I saw it now.

'Oh!' she said. She could hardly talk. 'You're so bitter, your mind is all warped and distorted.'

Bannister snapped a twig with a noise like a pistol shot.

'Bitter!' he said. 'They wonder why I am bitter.'

He laughed, but his face froze the same instant. His jaw jutted out. He began talking to the waves.

'Because, knowing that each moment might be the last, I was eager to grasp the fruits before it was too late. And reaching out for them—' Here he did reach out, a long, bony hand – 'What happened?'

He wasn't asking us, but the waves.

'A shell, a burst of red – the whole sky whirling red – blackness – a twisted leg – the fruits denied.'

He snatched back his hand.

'Bitter!' he said.

Mrs Bannister's face was darker even than his.

'If you're so bitter,' she ground out, taking her time. 'I wonder you go on living at all.'

That seemed to bring him out of the liquor a little.

'What, exactly, do you mean?' he demanded.

She picked up her things and started toward the car. I thought for a moment that maybe she was crying, and jumped up to help her.

Bannister half rose and then sank back, looking after her. You could tell his leg was paining him.

'Elsa, for God's sake!' he called. 'You don't mean—'

She turned very slowly and came back to look down at him. She wasn't crying.

'Has it honestly never occurred to you,' she said quietly, almost sadly, 'that you might be better – off – dead?'

It all seemed crazy, somehow – Grisby wanting to be 'killed,' offering me five thousand for the job – Bannister brooding about his twisted leg, bitter and defiant – his wife, years younger, who hated him, I knew now, and who made me suck in my breath each time I thought of us out on the raft—

I couldn't help wondering what I was letting myself in for. And almost at once I knew.

V

'Well, did you think it over?' Grisby asked. He was absolutely overflowing with enthusiasm and good cheer.

I told him yes. Yes, I said, except that I couldn't think of any motive I'd have for killing him.

'Motive!' he said. 'Is that all that's worrying you!'

He laughed. He patted me on the back. He was feeling good about something, all right.

It was dark – he'd stayed for dinner with the Bannisters. We were parked on a little hill just off the road leading to the station. Below was the swamp that ran beside the tracks and over the swamp was a purple haze, damp and sticky.

I'd heard that the place was a breeding ground for rats, as bad as Rats Island off the Harbor. No one lived out at this end; Bannister's was one of the last houses before you hit the swamp, and it was some way back. A few skeletons of buildings out on the dry places of the swamp showed where people had tried to make a go of it from time to time – small factories that had come out because the rent was cheap and the railroad near. They'd done everything to get rid of the rats and the ruins told who had won. It was some place.

I said: 'It's a cinch we can't use robbery. And what else is there? I'll have to tell them something, won't I?'

'The police? Sure. But who said anything about robbery?' His heavy brows worked up and down. 'You just leave everything to me, didn't I tell you? Good old Lee Grisby – an answer for everything. And the answer here? Accident, my boy, accident.'

'Accident!'

'Sure. Why not?'

I did some fast thinking.

'Well', I said, 'it might be an accident, my plugging you, but what would I be doing throwing your body in the Sound?'

'That's simple. You've heard of hit-and-run drivers, haven't you?'

I blinked.

I said: 'Now I suppose I'm to run over you, too. And then put a bullet through you. And then throw you in the Sound. Boy, you sure would be dead!'

He laughed again, really pleased. He said no, that wasn't the idea at all.

'The idea,' he said, 'is that you kill me accidentally. Then you get scared. You think maybe they won't believe you, or that there'll be hell to pay, or that even if you get off, you'll lose your job because of it. It's the same way driving, if you hit someone. Well, so you run. But in this case, you're going to take the precaution of disposing of the body.'

'So I throw you in the Sound?'

'Right. You're thinking this way, "If I don't, the police will ask why I took him to that lonely spot, and not to the station, as ordered. They'll say I tried to rob him, he fought and I killed him. No, better to get the body out of the way. Then no one will be the wiser."'

I was beginning to get scared all over again.

'What lonely spot?' I asked.

'The beach – Bannister's beach. Here's what happens. I come out to see Bannister. When I leave, you drive me to the station, just as usual. It's night, and we miss the train – we'll time it so we do.'

'So far so good. But I still don't see how I happen to shoot you.'

'I'm coming to that . . . Well, when we miss the train, we decide it's too hot to wait for the next one there at the station, so we go down to the beach to cool off. While we're waiting, we hear a sound. We think it might be a stick-up. You take the gun out of the side-pocket of the car – Bannister gave you one to carry, didn't he? That was my idea; I got him to do that. That just shows how careful I've been.

'All right. You start to get out of the car, to investigate, with the gun in your hand. The gun goes off, accidentally. It will, too, we'll see to that. Then you find I'm hit, get scared, and dump the body off the pier.'

'But not really,' I said.

He drew back and looked at me.

'It better *not* be really,' he said.

I had him there.

'But you said we'd have witnesses,' I reminded him.

'Sure we will. We've got to have. Otherwise how could we make it look like I was dead? Without a body, that takes a bit of proving.

People have to see us go down to the beach together. We'll make sure they do. Then people have to see *you* go back from the beach *alone*. That will be easy. There are always people around a beach on a hot night.'

I couldn't think of anything to say.

I said: 'How do you know it will be hot?'

'We'll pick a night that is . . . All right. They'll hear the shot. When they come running, you'll be alone. Why? Because enough time will elapse supposedly, for you to have disposed of the body. If not, if they come too soon, you can claim that you covered me over in the car and then disposed of the body after they left.'

'And what was I supposed to be shooting at?'

'The moon – a tin can – what do you care? You won't be trying to prove anything at this time except that you're alone. Later on, when the police start investigating, you'll break down and confess the accident. They'll check that. The witnesses will tell about us going down to the beach together and you going back alone. They'll tell about the shot. And everything will be just dandy.'

'And supposing they don't believe it was an accident?'

'Supposing they don't? We went over that. They've got to produce the body . . . Well, does that answer the burning question of the hour? Or is there something else? Ask me if there is. There can't be any slip up. This has got to go off like clockwork.'

I felt pretty miserable.

I said: 'Well, they might send me to jail just to make sure I didn't go around killing anyone else.'

'Don't be silly. I told you they couldn't hold you. Any dumb lawyer could get you out. But we covered all that, too. What else is there?'

'One big question is: When?'

Grisby took off his glasses and began wiping them with a crisp white handkerchief.

'When?' he said. 'Soon. Very soon. Maybe tomorrow night.'

He looked out where the moonlight ripped the haze over the swamp, thinking.

'You mean it?' I asked.

'Why not?'

'I hadn't figured—'

'Why wait? Once I hit on a plan and see that it's air-tight, I go ahead. Yes, sir,' he said, 'I think tomorrow night!'

'But why tomorrow night, especially?'

'The papers say it's going to be hot tomorrow night. We've got to be sure of our witnesses.'

I didn't trust him. Something was wrong somewhere.

'As far as that goes,' I said, 'it's plenty hot tonight. Why not tonight?'

He squirmed around to look at me in the light from the dash. Something in the way he looked chilled me. Gooseflesh stood out on my arms.

'Something's itching you,' he said. 'What is it?'

His voice was as raw as the mist that crawled beside the car.

I said: 'Nothing at all. Why?'

'You aren't still worrying about the motive?'

'Oh, no.'

'Then what is it?'

'Why—'

'Come on, out with it!'

I had to say it then: 'It just doesn't seem that you've told me everything.'

He kept on looking at me for a minute and then sank back. That gave me a chance to light a cigarette and pull myself together. I'd been scared for a minute there, I'll admit it. Now I felt all right again, and he seemed just like he always did. I might have imagined that he'd been different.

He stroked his big full jaw, holding his eyeglasses in the other hand and tapping them on his knee, thinking. He was pretty good-looking with his glasses off. His short, wiry gold hair, actor's profile and powerful build probably had made him a devil with the women when he was young. Maybe still, for all I knew.

'I can't think of anything I've left out,' he said. 'Unless – yes, of course. The five thousand. I don't blame you! Well, let's see. Bannister and his wife are going into town tomorrow. She's going shopping – you can drop her somewhere, leave him at the office and then run over to the bank with me. You can see me draw the money out. In fact, I'll give you some in advance. That's fair enough, isn't it?'

'Oh, that part of it is all right. I didn't mean that.'

'No? Then—'

'Well,' I said, 'it's the reason for all this. You said it was to get rid of your wife. You want her to think you're dead. That's all right; she won't give you a divorce, and if you want to get away from everything, anyway, like you said, why not?'

'That's your answer, isn't it? I tell you, Laurence, a man can stand only so much. Some jump off buildings, some join the Foreign Legion, but I have more imagination. I adopt a new and exciting identity and come up in the South Seas!'

'I know, and I'm all for it. I just don't see why you should go to all this trouble, and give me five thousand dollars, just to do that. What's to stop you from just going, I mean? She couldn't stop you, that's a cinch. And there's no law against it, that I know of.'

He smiled.

'I said you were smart. You are. But do you suppose she'd let me desert her without a struggle? She'd follow me to the ends of the earth, just to make life miserable for me, if nothing else. No, better to make it final. Let her think I'm dead. Let everyone think I'm dead. Do the job up right.'

It still seemed fishy to me, somehow, but I couldn't put my finger on it.

He went on: 'Don't you suppose I've thought it all over, nights lying awake when I couldn't sleep for worry? Don't you see that it's worth something to me in peace of mind to know that my whole past is finished? You're young; maybe you don't see. Let's hope you never do!'

'Well—'

He couldn't figure me out. I couldn't either, but there was a red light flashing in front of me that said, 'Stop!'

'I guess you don't want that five thousand very badly,' he said. 'I guess you get offers like that every day.'

I said: 'No, I don't. I want the money, all right, who wouldn't, but I think you better count me out.'

'What!'

'I don't think I want to go through with it,' I said.

VI

I had to see where I stood, for one thing. I wasn't half as sure of myself as I sounded. And as for that, I knew pretty well where I stood, too. Right behind the eight ball.

'Why, you can't back out now,' he said.

He wasn't trying to scare me. It was a plain statement of fact, the way he said it.

I looked out over the swamp. The corners of my mouth were twitching. I didn't want him to see me that way.

'Why not?' I asked. My voice shook.

'"Why not?"' he echoed. 'Jesus! Use your head. Where would I be? You're in this thing and you've got to go through with it.'

'I know, but—'

He laughed, but not like he usually did. This one gave me the shivers all over again.

'I thought you were tough. I thought you had your eye on the main chance. You're not going to break down and cry, are you? I'm not even asking you to *do* anything for the five thousand, just make it look as though you'd killed me. Why, I could get the real thing done for a century note, or half that much.'

'That's just it. It's like you said. You can get someone else to do it for nothing, almost. Why give me five thousand?'

'Why not? I've taken an interest in you, I've got plenty of money to last me, you're doing me a favor, and after tomorrow night we'll probably never see each other again. So why figure there must be a catch to it?'

'I don't. I'm just not sure that's all there is to it.'

He gave a snort. I was getting him mad, but I had to find out.

'You mean you're scared,' he said. 'A hell of a fine sailor you make! What kind of a ship were you on, anyway, a ferry boat? Look at your hands. They're shaking!'

I stuck to the point: 'You haven't told me all of it.'

'Why should I tell you anything? You'd break down and cry when the time came. You'd blab it all. You'd spill your guts the first chance you got.' He looked me up and down. 'Boy,' he said, 'you're a pip. How I ever came to think you had guts in the first place is a mystery to me.'

'Nuts. You'd shake too, if someone started that kind of talk with you. What is this? Of course I've got to know it all. I'd be in a sweet jam if I didn't and something went wrong. So would you be. But if you really feel that way about it, all right!'

I slammed in the clutch.

'No, wait a minute.'

He put a hand on my arm to stop me, and then I saw that he was smiling.

'Now you're talking sense,' he said. 'I didn't think I'd made a mistake in you, but I had to test you out, didn't I? All right. Now I'll give it to you – both barrels.'

When he did I almost collapsed.

'Everything I told you stands,' he said. 'I disappear. You go back to your work as though nothing had happened. The police come for you. They don't know about me yet, don't even know I've disappeared. It's too early for that.'

'Then what are they coming after me for?'

He lowered his voice.

'They're coming for you for another killing, not mine.'

I sucked in my breath. My ears were ringing. So that was it! *Another* killing. I knew there was a catch somewhere. This was it!

Grisby ran on:

'They question you – accuse you of the murder. You break down under their grilling. As far as you're concerned, it's anything to get out of the rap. You take a long chance. You prove you *couldn't* have done the other *by confessing to killing me*. I said you'd be anxious enough to prove it when the time came. Here's why. By proving you killed *me* – accidentally, just as we planned it – you prove you couldn't have done the other.'

'Why not?'

'*Because that will be twenty miles away, at about the same time.* Well, then they'll drop the other – they'll have to, you can see that – and try to get you for killing me. Do you follow? And of course they can't get to first base there because they can't produce the body. So you're free and you've got five thousand dollars salted away that they can't touch.'

I said: 'Why would they figure I'd killed someone twenty mile away?'

'Because I'll see that they do. I'll see that they think it's a lead-pipe cinch that you did it. *That's* what you're getting your five thousand for. First, to throw them off the track. Second, to establish the fact of my death.'

I gulped.

'But don't worry,' he said. 'I could leave your cap – hell, I could leave your picture there – and they still couldn't do anything. Not so long as you can prove that you were killing me and dumping me off the pier, and can account for your time afterwards. Now do you see? Your part is simple and foolproof. You're safe every minute of the time and you don't have to slap anyone's wrist, even, to get your five thousand.'

'You mean *you're* going to be killing someone – twenty miles away – while I'm supposed to be killing you?'

'At about the same time, yes.'

'How will you do that?'

'That's easy. Speedboat – East River. I've clocked it. I can get from the beach out here to where I want to go – the foot of Wall Street – in twenty-five to thirty minutes. The reason is, it's shorter and faster by water than it is by land.'

'Oh.'

'Now you know the real reason for my wanting to be dead, as far as the police are concerned. How can I be off killing someone else if I'm dead myself and at the bottom of the Sound? Of course, being dead also frees me from my wife, which I want, and lets me go down to the South Seas, which I want, and lets me get hold of a nice little sum, which I want.'

I got my wind.

I said: 'Who – who's the one you—'

He narrowed his eyes and leaned forward until his face was close to mine. He gripped my arm – hard.

'That doesn't concern you,' he said. 'But I'll tell you because I agree you should know all the angles, it's best, and because it won't do you a damn bit of good to talk. No one would believe you, in the first place.' His grip on my arm tightened. 'And in the second place, if you did, they'd still have nothing on me. You haven't any proof. And in the third place, you wouldn't, because if you didn't go through with this now, you know damned well I'd fog you – and as easily as I will him!'

He let that sink in a minute, and then he said quickly:

'Bannister.'

VII

Twenty minutes later I was back in my room, shaking like I had the palsy.

I was getting out of there. Fast. If I didn't go now it would be too late. There wouldn't be any backing down. He'd get me too, just as he'd said he would. I'd be a dead one. I knew it.

I started furiously cramming everything I had into a duffle bag. I hadn't much.

It was about eleven o'clock. Hot and still. They wouldn't be wanting the car any more until morning. By then I'd be far away.

A breeze was up off the Sound. It came in through the window and rustled things.

I looked out and saw the water. Far off the lights of a ship moved out to the open sea.

Then I knew what I was going to do – sign back on a ship – go to sea!

I was packed. There wasn't a thing to hold me. I thought of going and telling Bannister the whole thing. He'd been swell to me. But I didn't go. I didn't want any part of it.

I slung the duffle over my shoulder.

A knock came at the door. My heart leaped.

Grisby!

But it couldn't be – it couldn't! I'd seen him take the train, just a little while before. Who, then? For a panicky moment I thought maybe it was the police already.

'Who's there?' I called.

'May I come in?' A slurred voice – one I didn't know.

It was a young fellow I'd never seen before. He was stoop-shouldered,

27

slack-jawed, with watery blue eyes and smoky gray hair that didn't go with the rest of him. He was wearing pleated gray slacks and a blue polo shirt.

'You Larry Planter?' he asked.

I nodded.

'Why?'

'My name's Broome,' he said. 'I'm the new gardener. They told me you'd fix me up. Mind if I sit down?'

'Not at all. You found your room?'

'Oh, yes, Mrs Bannister showed me.'

He sat down on the edge of the bed and began to roll a cigarette.

'She's a honey,' he said.

He fired up and leaned back like he was going to spend the night.

I sat down at my desk and lighted up too. I was plenty jittery still, but I didn't know how to get rid of the guy.

'Nice room you got here. Mine's a little small.' His room was down the hall, at the end. There were only the two rooms. 'But I'm glad for the job, I sure am.'

'Been a gardener long?'

'Well, not a plain gardener, no. I studied landscaping architecture for years. But take my advice – don't ever get in it. Business is rotten. You don't look like a chauffeur.'

'I'm not, but I've always monkeyed with cars. What does a chauffeur look like?'

'I mean, you look too smart. No offense.'

'Oh, no. I was just curious.'

He looked at the books and the papers on the writing desk.

'You write?'

'Some.'

'Boy, I could sure give you a lot of good material. I've run into some mighty funny situations, going around. Mostly out at these rich Long Island places. Take this one. You can see plain as the wart on my face' – he had one, too – 'that Bannister is poison to his wife. I'll just bet she'd be willing to play, given half a chance.'

I decided right there I didn't like him. He was too stuck on himself. Why, she wouldn't even look at him.

28

'You've got her wrong,' I said.

'Maybe you just don't know how to handle women. I've seen her around off and on for months. She used to drop in at the Innes place down the road. I was doing a job there she liked and she said to come over here when I got through. That was a break, but don't tell me she's only interested in my flowers. Ever try?'

'She isn't that sort,' I said.

'You just don't know how to handle 'em.' He blew out smoke. 'Me, I know. They're all alike. Of course, not if they're already in love. You have to know if there's someone else in the picture. I don't mean the husband. He doesn't count.'

He wrinkled his nose and looked wise.

'You drive her around,' he said. 'Maybe there's someone in the city—?'

'Not a chance,' I said. 'You've got her wrong.'

He pursed his lips and made lines in his forehead.

'Well, maybe,' he said. He had a sudden inspiration. 'Say, how'd you like a drink? I'll go get it. Be right back.'

He went out to the other room and came back with the bottle. It was cheap whiskey but just what I needed. We had a couple of quick ones and then he poured some in glasses and sat down.

'How about this guy Grisby?' he asked.

'What do you mean?'

'He comes out here a lot, doesn't he? You don't suppose he comes out just to see Bannister?'

'Why not? They're partners.'

'Yeah, I know.'

'You know a lot, it seems to me.'

'Oh, I hear things. Remember, I've been working this territory for a couple of years now.'

'What did you mean by that crack about Grisby?'

'Not a thing. I mean I know the set-up. Bannister and his bum leg. A beautiful wife. His partner, Grisby— Hell, I don't know. What do you mean?'

I downed the drink. I began to feel a little high.

'Nothing,' I said. 'But you're wrong.'

'Well, you can never tell, as the saying goes.'

He threw his cigarette into the open fireplace and began to roll another.

I got up and stretched.

'Well, you're all set for the night, if she showed you the room,' I said. 'Anything you want to know, just ask me tomorrow. I'm going to turn in. Had a hard day.'

'Sure, sure.' He stood up. 'I don't need a house to fall on me.'

'Oh, I didn't mean—'

'No offense. How about another drink before hitting the hay – just to show we're friends?'

We each had a stiff one.

'Go ahead, kill it,' he said.

I emptied the bottle. The stuff had a wallop.

'Well, see you in the morning,' he said. He went out walking like he was a little tight.

I knew damned well that I was. It was dumb to drink in hot weather – cheap whiskey, at that. I sat down and put my head in my hands. This was a fine stew I'd got myself in, all right, all right. I could hardly believe it was me. I went over and over the whole thing.

Then I did it. I sat down at the desk and began to write. I spilled my guts, as Grisby said I would.

I wrote:

'O.K., Mr Bannister! You've been a good guy. Here's where I pay you back. I ran into this thing without knowing what was coming, so don't hold it against me. Here's the dope – all of it . . .'

And I gave it to him. All of it. Just as Grisby'd given it to me, white hot off the griddle.

It was after twelve by the time I was through. I could hear Broome snoring in the other room. Good. I left the note on the writing desk where they'd be sure to see it in the morning and hauled the duffle out from under the bed.

At the door I took one last look at the room, switched off the light, and went out without making a sound. It had been swell while it lasted.

The phone rang.

I stood on the steps with the bag in my hand and listened. If I hadn't waited to write the note I'd have been out and away. I wouldn't have heard the phone. Why answer it now?

Broome hadn't heard it, evidently. In between the rings I could still hear him snoring.

The phone stopped ringing. It was suddenly so quiet I could hear crickets chirping far off.

I went on down the steps. At the bottom, my hand on the knob, I stopped. There was a crunching of gravel just outside.

Someone was coming!

I stood still, the sweat pouring out of me.

The sound stopped outside the door. The door opened.

In the moonlight stood Elsa Bannister.

VIII

She was wearing a filmy thing that floated out and around her like a mist. In the moonlight it seemed that she was floating too.

I came out and put the bag down on the drive, not looking at her any more than I could help.

'Well, Laurence—' she began.

'Yes'm?'

'The phone – didn't you hear it?'

I scrunched the gravel with my foot.

'You're not – you're not thinking of going away?' she asked, surprised.

I nodded.

'Well, Laurence—' She didn't know what to make of it. 'But you can't,' she said. 'We like you here. You don't mean you have a better offer? Is that it? But I'm sure, if you spoke to Mr Bannister—'

'It isn't that,' I said. 'It's just that I wasn't cut out for a chauffeur.'

'But you make a very good one, really. At least, we're satisfied, and that's the main thing, isn't it?'

'Not to me. I mean, the life's too slow. Maybe you didn't know it, but I was a sailor before I came here. I'm going back where I belong.'

'I think I see what you mean,' she said slowly. 'But hadn't you better think it over?'

'I have thought it over,' I said.

'Oh . . .' She came closer. 'You've been drinking, haven't you? Come, be sensible. I couldn't sleep, it was so hot. I thought a drive might help. We'll run down to the beach and in the morning everything will look different to you, I'm sure.'

'Well—'

I got the car out.

I was feeling the liquor pretty much but I could drive fine. We went out along the Sound and watched the moonlight on the water. All the while music kept running through my head. It was all very beautiful.

We had been riding about an hour when she tapped me on the shoulder.

'You can go back now.'

That was all she had said on the whole ride.

I turned the car around. There was no one else on the road at this hour and it seemed there was no one else in the world. I'd forgotten Grisby. I'd forgotten everything except that we were alone together and that it was a wonderful feeling.

When we came to the side road leading down to the beach, she said:

'This is fine – just drive in here.'

I ran the car to the edge of a hill that sloped down to the sand of the beach. A few fires were still burning but there was no one around. We might as well have been on a desert island.

She got out and stretched her arms above her head, looking up at the stars.

'It's a glorious night,' she said – to herself, not to me.

I stood next to her. My nose burned from the scent of her hair. She was wearing sandals and seemed smaller than she had and more like a girl. I wasn't afraid of her any more, anyway.

'If you want that big red one now,' I said, 'I think I can get it for you.'

She smiled, looking up at me with her lips parted and her teeth very white. The look had surprise in it. I guessed it was her turn now to see me for the first time – really see me, I mean.

'You have a romantic mind, for a chauffeur,' she said.

'I told you, I'm not a chauffeur. I'm a sailor, I've been all around the world.'

'You were in the Navy?'

'No. I was on tramp steamers.'

'Oh.'

She went on down the bank. At the bottom was a little hollow made in the sand. There she stopped.

'Bring the robe down, won't you?' she asked.

I got it out of the car and came down and spread it out for her in the sand.

'Sit down,' she said.

I dropped down beside her and watched the waves roll up the shore. She was too close for me to think of anything but her, but I didn't want to look at her. I was afraid I might do something silly.

We were very quiet. After a while she leaned back with her hands behind her head and began to recite a poem. It made me go hot and cold:

> 'Deep on the couch of night a siren star,
>   Steeping cold earth in swooning loveliness,
>   Sings madness to the earthlings that we are . . .'

I looked down at her lying with the stars in her eyes. A smile almost sad was coming and going at her lips.

'That is how I feel about tonight,' she said, and added, 'You're very quiet. Talk to me.'

I thought, why not? This is the last night. If I was ever going to seize the moment, as Bannister said, it was now. Bannister was right, the moment might never come again. With the whiskey and all, it never occurred to me how funny it was, using his own stuff on his wife.

I said: 'I'll tell you something that might interest you. I wouldn't do it, except I'm leaving.'

'What is that?' she asked. She knew what was coming, all right. Her eyes opened wider, but she didn't try to stop me.

I took the plunge.

'If you weren't married—' I began.

'Oh!'

'That makes a difference, I know, but—'

'It makes a tremendous difference,' she said.

I was feeling the liquor pretty much, all right, or I never would have said it.

I said: 'But every woman should have a husband and a lover, shouldn't she?'

She didn't seem too surprised.

'But it's impossible, you must see that.'

I pretended to think that over. Then I gave it everything I had, all the things I remembered out of books.

I said: 'I don't see why. A woman might dream over a book, mightn't she, when her husband is away? She could imagine, couldn't she, that the lover in the book was her lover? Women do that in theaters. I will be your theater! I'll bring you love, romance, glamour – everything you'd get in a theater! Say that you're in a theater now, or that you're reading a book—'

The funny thing about it was that that's just where I'd got it – out of a book.

'Ah, but this isn't a book,' she said. 'And it isn't a theater.'

'Sure,' I said, 'I know. And I'm only a chauffeur. At least, that's what you think.'

'No, I can't say that I do, entirely – not any more. But you certainly aren't a character in a book.'

'Then say it's a dream and forget the book. It's all right for a woman to dream, isn't it?'

'It might be all right in a book, as you say, but not in real life.'

We were talking like high school kids, but we both knew it, and we both knew that it was only a matter of minutes now.

'Maybe it would be wrong in real life, yes,' I said, 'but this isn't real. This is a dream. Tomorrow it will be like something that never happened. Don't forget, I'll be gone, then, too – that will make it even more like a dream.'

'Yes, I know . . . but it isn't right.'

I went ahead full steam.

'It's not happening, either,' I said. 'It's a dream. Didn't I tell you?'

I kissed her mouth. It was a nice little kiss, like you'd give a child. I was afraid I'd scare her, otherwise.

When I stopped she kept her eyes closed. I looked at her lying in the moonlight. I put an arm under her and this time kissed her hard. A shiver ran through her; her lips parted. It lasted a long time and it felt just as it must feel drowning – drifting under water.

Suddenly she put a hand on my chest and pushed me back. She sat up, looking around, her eyes blurred. I felt the same way, as though I'd been asleep.

'You said a dream,' she whispered.

She looked flushed and excited, more like a girl. I smoothed the hair from her forehead and ran my fingers through it until it hung down her back. She threw back her head, leaning on both hands, and let her hair fall in ripples to the sand. She looked at the stars.

I lay back and looked at them, too. The sky seemed filled with star-shells and sky-rockets, all bursting and throwing out sparks.

'It's late,' she said. 'It's very late. We must hurry back.'

'Why?'

'Because we must. There will be other nights.'

'No,' I said.

'Of course there will be.'

'No. I'm quitting.'

'But you can't quit now.' She looked at me like no one else had ever looked before. 'It is amazing, but—'

'What?'

She lowered her eyes. She bit the corner of her lip.

'I have been unhappy,' she said. She raised her eyes. 'I am not unhappy now. That is the amazing thing.'

Her eyes were veiled over. Her cheeks were wet.

She came into my arms as though she had been there always. I kissed her throat, the shadow made by the curve of her breasts. She trembled. I drew back and looked at her. Her eyes were closed. Her hands came up and drew my head down to hers. My mouth touched hers.

I struck the roof of the sky. It was only a kiss, but like none I'd ever had before.

I came down with a crash like the crashing of waves in my ear, and my whole body shaking and my breath coming in gasps that burned my throat. Sand, sky, Sound, all whirled around me.

'Laurence!'

She sprang up, pulling the negligee around her, and ran stumbling and falling up the hill.

I got up on one knee. I was weak, shaking.

Then I saw her . . . on the hill . . . A moment, a second before I had held her in my arms, had run hot hands across her body. Now she was up on the hill. I started climbing hand and knee.

'Wait . . . you're forgetting the robe.'

That brought me out of it a little. I stood up and looked dumbly back at the robe for a minute. Then I went back and got it. Her handkerchief was there, with the kind of perfume she wore on it. I put it in my pocket.

At the house she kissed me again, trembling, happy, younger than ever.

'Tomorrow,' she whispered.

IX

I was still dazed when I got up to the room, after putting the car away.

I threw myself down on the bed. Even now I could feel her arms tight around me, her fingers pulling my hair, her perfume choking me. I could still hear her saying, in a whisper, 'Tomorrow!'

Suddenly I sat up, and there, on the desk, was the letter I'd written to warn Bannister – staring at me.

I couldn't stay, I knew that. I jumped to my feet and looked at the time. Three-thirty. I could be far away by morning.

'Tomorrow!'

No, I'd go in the morning. Early. Before anyone else was up. Then there would be cars on the road. I could get a ride into the city. I'd go right down to the Battery and sign up on a ship. Anywhere.

I couldn't sleep. I lay and tossed. I saw her a thousand times, a thousand ways. She was right in the room with me. Every minute. Smiling. Crying. Pushing me back. Pulling me down to her . . .

I couldn't stand it. I got up and dressed. I hauled the duffle bag out again . . . put in some things I'd forgotten. Then I went back and tossed on the bed some more. Still I couldn't sleep. I lay and tossed.

A light broke across the sky. Day was coming . . . at last, at last.

I sat up with a jerk. *This was the day*. In the writhing early light I could see Grisby, standing with the gun smoking in his hand. I could see Bannister . . . a hole in his head . . . the blood streaming down his face . . .

MURDER!

I grabbed the bag. I went out of there like a shot.

At the bottom of the steps, I stopped. I thought of her standing out there, in the moonlight outside the door . . . floating . . . saying, surprised, 'Why, Laurence – you're not – you're not going away—' The way she had when I'd come down before.

I put my hand on the knob and leaned against the wall. My heart beating wildly, just like then. The sweat pouring out of me . . .

Suddenly I smelled her perfume again. Strong. As though she were standing out there – as though she were in my arms again, her body pressing, her breath coming fast, her lips trembling, her perfume choking me.

'But you can't quit now . . .'

It was the handkerchief. I took it out. It was lace, like her negligee. I put it to my mouth, my hand shaking, my temples throbbing.

'Tomorrow!'

But I couldn't stay. I couldn't see Bannister killed like that, in cold blood.

I couldn't go, either. I thought of how it would be – Bannister gone, Elsa alone, five thousand dollars in my pocket. And I thought of Elsa – Elsa saying, quietly, 'Has it honestly never occurred to you' – speaking to Bannister – 'that you might be better off dead?'

I shoved the handkerchief into my pocket.

It wouldn't be my doing. *I* wasn't going to kill anyone. If Bannister couldn't watch out for himself, it was his own fault. It was that kind of a world. You had to be looking out for yourself all the time, every minute.

Anyway, Grisby had threatened to kill me if I didn't do what he said, hadn't he? And it wasn't a bluff, it was the real thing, I knew it. I could still hear him:

'It won't do you a damn bit of good to talk. No one would believe you in the first place. And in the second place, if you did, they'd still have nothing on me. You haven't any proof. And in the third place, you wouldn't, because if you didn't go through with this now, you know damned well I'd fog you – and as easily as I will him!'

I couldn't imagine myself going through with it, but it didn't seem that all this was happening to me, either, but to somebody else. And I couldn't do anything about it. It was like walking in your sleep – and having a nightmare of being on a precipice, with someone ready to push you off into the bargain.

I went back up the steps to the room. I took the note I'd written to warn Bannister and tore it into pieces. I put the pieces in the fireplace. I struck a match to them.

They blazed up with a roar – a bright, hot flame.

I shivered.

I threw myself down on the bed and this time I went to sleep. And the last thing I thought of was Elsa – Elsa whispering hotly:

'Tomorrow!'

PART TWO

I

Now it was starting! . . .

We were on the road that ran beside the swamp. We were going to the station to miss the train, and then to the beach for the 'murder.'

It was hot.

My hands felt slack on the wheel of the car. I was all empty inside. My eyes were blurred from the heat. I felt as though I really were going to kill someone.

It was dark.

Clouds hung low in the sky.

Now and then there was lightning. It came in sheets, moving half across the sky. It lighted the clouds. Then the clouds were like sheep going to the slaughter.

But there was no rain. There was not even the usual cool prelude to rain. It was more sticky, more sultry than ever.

Grisby leaned over and looked at his watch in the light from the dash.

'Ten-thirty,' he said. 'We'll have to hurry. The train must be gone by this time anyway.'

The train was late. We heard its whistle wailing over the swamp, and then we saw the lights of it through the haze, coming toward the station. If we kept going the way we were, we'd get there just as the train did. That would be bad, if anybody saw us. The idea was to just miss it.

My hands were shaky. My eyes were heavy. I watched the blur of the train's lights. For a moment I forgot to watch the road.

Suddenly I saw a red light. It seemed to be coming of itself, directly toward my face.

39

Grisby yelled. His voice sounded far away, more angered than afraid.

'Stop the car! Stop the—'

He lurched forward in the seat and jerked back the emergency.

I swung the wheel around. I jammed on the foot brakes.

Too late.

There was a stunning crash. Glass showered me. I was thrown forward against the wheel. I gasped.

The car stopped.

I tasted blood on my lips, hot and salty. I opened the car door and slid out.

Now I saw that what I had hit was a truck. It was covered with black tarpaulin. A little man in a cap leaped out of the truck and came up running.

'Anybody hurt?' he asked.

'Why – I don't know—'

We looked in the car. Grisby was getting out on the other side. He came around the back. When he stood beside the little man he looked like a giant. Blood was on his white linen suit. He was smiling, but one hand was holding his right wrist.

'Well, that was a narrow one, wasn't it?' he said. 'Not hurt, are you, Laurence?'

'I don't know. The glass—'

'Flying glass can take your head off,' said the little man.

We moved into the light from the twisted headlights and examined our cuts. The whole front of the car was jammed against the back of the truck. What I had seen had been the truck's red tail-light. Now the light was out. Except for that, the truck didn't seem to be damaged.

Grisby had a cut on his right wrist. It was deep. Blood ran out of it in a stream.

I felt faint. I wasn't hurt, only scratched. But the sight of the blood nauseated me, knowing what we were going to do.

The little man was looking at Grisby's wrist.

'Maybe you cut the jugular vein,' he said. 'Or is that in the neck?'

Grisby laughed. He wrapped a handkerchief around the wrist and knotted it with his teeth. Then he smiled, to show that he was all right.

'Is the car O.K.?' asked the little man.

We pushed it clear of the truck. I got in and started the motor. It ran fine.

The radiator was crushed in, but there didn't seem to be a leak anywhere. The radiator ornament was missing. I found it in the dust of the road. It was Atlas holding the world. Now it was only Atlas, flattened out of shape. The world wasn't anywhere around. I threw the rest away.

Grisby wheeled on the little man.

'What's your name?' he demanded. It sounded like a prosecutor questioning a defendant.

The truck driver gaped.

'You're not going to say that *I* did this!'

'Oh, no. It was entirely our fault. We want to make sure that you're compensated for any damage we may have caused your truck. That's all.'

'Well, that's different. My name's Steve Crunch. It'd be my job if I had to take the rap for this.'

'Don't I know it,' I said. 'I used to drive one of these crates myself.'

'Then you know how it is. You can be as careful as a preacher on his wedding night, but let something happen that wasn't your fault at all, and you're done for.'

Grisby laughed. He gave the little man one of his cards.

'Let me know the damage,' he said.

The little man took the card. On the plain side he wrote down the license number of Bannister's car.

II

Now we were on the road leading to Bannister's beach.

Grisby chuckled.

'Everything is working out perfectly,' he said. 'That truck driver will make a Grade-A witness. But now we'll have to work faster than ever. Bannister is waiting for me down at the office. I got him to stay down for the night; the case we're working on comes up tomorrow.'

'Does he know you're out here?'

'Oh, yes. I accidentally on purpose left the most important papers on the case out here last night. His leg is bothering him and he's irritable as hell, so he was glad to have me go after them and leave him to suffer alone. Well, his leg won't bother him any more after tonight.'

We stopped at the top of the little hill that sloped down to the beach.

There were fires all up and down. When the lightning spread across the sky we could see people moving. There was a stir and excitement in the air.

Someone was singing. I thought of Elsa in my arms on the beach. I felt the blood rush to my head. Again I smelled her perfume. The handkerchief was still in my pocket. I reached in and felt the lace, cool on my fingers.

A couple came along, walking slowly.

'Wait till they pass,' said Grisby.

It was dark on the beach in front of the car. They stopped and kissed. Then they went on.

Grisby got out and untied the handkerchief from his wrist. He let the blood run onto the seat and the floor.

'What are you doing?' I almost screamed. My voice sounded strange, choked.

'Use your head. You can't shoot someone and not expect some blood. Get out the gun.'

I reached my hand into the side-pocket of the car. The gun handle was cold. I took the gun out.

'Didn't I tell you this was the perfect crime?' said Grisby. 'There isn't a detail I've overlooked. Even this blood here. They'll check it against a blood test I had made a week ago, in preparation.'

He began to give last minute instructions.

'Now, make sure someone sees you go back, when you leave here. Make sure of your witnesses, and that they know you're *alone*. When you get back to the garage, start washing out the bloodstains. You're trying to hide the evidence, see? But be careful not to do such a good job that they can't analyze the stains. To save your own neck, you've got to make sure they believe I'm dead.'

He reached over inside the car and smeared some blood on my trousers.

'Just try to wash that off,' he said.

He laughed as I drew back.

The singing made the whole thing seem even worse than it was.

My breathing was uneven. I tried to get hold of myself. I didn't look at Grisby. I kept my eyes on the beach. I could see the exact spot where the blanket had been last night. I could feel Elsa's hands running through my hair. My scalp tingled.

Grisby retied the handkerchief and tossed a packet of bills into my lap.

'Now, for God's sake, earn your salt,' he said. 'Play the game right. Act scared as hell. When they accuse you of killing Bannister, pretend to be surprised. Finally, break down and prove you couldn't have killed him by telling them about me. Stick to your story that you killed me. They can't do anything. Don't let them make you think they can.'

I leafed through the bills. I didn't count them . . . mostly fifties and hundreds, but some five-hundreds, I saw. More money than I'd ever held before in my life!

I didn't feel happy, however.

Some of the blood was on the bills, from my trousers. I quickly dropped the package onto the seat.

The gun handle began to feel hot. I could hardly hold it. My hands were wet and slippery with sweat.

Grisby reached over and grabbed my free hand.

'This is good-bye,' he said. 'Think of me down in the South Seas, happy for the first time in my life.'

I was so shaken up my hand was limp. Suddenly he dropped it in disgust. His jaw jutted out. He became a different Grisby, the killer. He leaned toward me.

'You go through with this like I told you,' he almost shouted, 'or I'll come back and get you, too. Now let that sink in, and sink in good. You can't be a kid all your life. Wake up and get some sense. You've got to be hard to get by in this world. Are you going to be hard, or should I finish you off right here?'

'I just don't feel well,' I said.

'All right, but no phony stuff, or I pop you.'

He went to the edge of the hill and looked up and down the beach.

'Now for it,' he said. 'As soon as you hear the speedboat die away, fire the gun.'

I saw his white linen suit going out on the pier. It made a good target. I could have taken the gun right then and killed him really. That would have saved Bannister, but then where would I have been? I might have thrown the body in the Sound, too, but how could I have been sure they wouldn't find it?

I sat up suddenly. The white suit was coming back!

I got out of the car in a hurry, the gun pointed forward. Maybe he knew I was thinking of killing him really!

He came up fuming.

'A little thing like this and I forget it,' he said. 'Quick, give me your cap!'

I gave it to him. Then he was gone again.

The speedboat made a terrific racket, but nobody seemed to pay any attention. They were used to such sounds.

Pretty soon the putt-putt died away. The singing came back clear.

I pointed the gun at the sand.

I pulled the trigger. The sound of the gun going off was so loud in my ears that I could hear it days after.

The singing stopped. For a second there was silence, while the smoke from the gun curled around my head. Then lightning swept the sky again and voices started shouting.

I didn't know whether to stand or run. My impulse was to hurl the gun into the sand.

I felt as though I had really killed someone with the shot. A feeling of guilt chilled me.

Then I snapped out of it. I hurried down to the pier, quickly started back again. People must see me coming up from the pier so they would think afterwards I threw the body in the Sound.

My heart was pounding.

The first man to come up was a fat man in a bathrobe. He grabbed the gun out of my hand. He was excited.

'Here, what are you doing?' he shouted.

Others came running, men and women.

'What happened?' they asked. 'What was the shooting for?'

I was suddenly very cool. I laughed and motioned to the gun.

'Why, I just felt like hearing it go off,' I said. 'Is there anything wrong in that?'

'Oh, you just did it for a whim, I suppose,' the fat man said.

'That's right,' I said. 'It was just a whim.'

Going back, I was surprised at how quiet everything was. Even the thunder seemed hushed and far away.

No one was around, either on the road or at the station. That was bad – the idea was that people should see me going back from the beach alone. It was part of the plan, to prove I couldn't have been down on Wall Street.

But nobody saw me.

It was dark on the road beside the swamp. A cold mist rose and fell in the light from the headlamps. I drove slowly, watching the road through the haze, my eyes smarting.

Suddenly the lights on the car went out. Blackness rushed in, blotting out the road.

I slammed on the brakes and got out to have a look. The road here dropped sharply to the swamp, a ten-foot fall. It was impossible to go on in the dark.

I found the flashlight and looked for the break in the wiring. It must have happened in the accident, and for some reason had held together until now. But I couldn't find it and at last had to give it up. All I could do was wait for the moonlight to come through – and after a while it did, just long enough for me to make the garage.

III

Now it was over.

I was back in my room over the garage.

The first thing I had to do was hide the money.

I didn't want to touch it. That was silly. I hadn't done anything. Yet I felt guilty.

Perhaps it was the blood. Grisby's blood. It was just as though I had killed him really, and had taken his money.

I tried not to think of Grisby, or of Bannister.

The clock was ticking. I was surprised to see that it was only eleven-thirty. I thought if it hadn't been for the lights going out, I'd have been back by eleven.

I looked for a likely spot to hide the money. No place seemed safe; the police were sure to find it. Each place I thought of seemed the one they would look first.

At last I decided on the mattress. I took my knife and cut a slit along the bottom, just large enough for the package. It went in nicely.

A sound startled me. I whirled to face the door. A quick spasm of shaking seized me.

The door was opening.

In the doorway stood Broome, smiling sickly. He was wearing the same blue polo shirt and gray slacks. His hair was rumpled.

I smoothed down the covers and then turned them up again as though I were getting ready for bed. My blood was racing. I thought there was guilt all over my face.

'Are you home?' he asked. Silly question.

What I said was just as silly. I had forgotten it was not yet late. I had thought it was; even though I had just seen the clock, my impression that it was late remained.

'What are you doing wandering around at this hour?'

He came into the room. 'As the college professor said, "My eyes are prominent and pink; My mouth tastes like the kitchen sink; I am not well."'

I started to laugh, he looked so funny reciting the poem. But my lips wouldn't take the laugh.

'You mean you've been drinking?' I asked.

'Um-huh . . . like a little drink yourself?'

'No, thanks, I'm going to bed.'

'Well, good-night,' he said. He squinted and looked at my trousers, then at the cuts on my face.

'Say—'

'Oh, that. Just a little accident,' I told him.

'Accident?' He could hardly say the word.

'Yes. In the car. Nothing serious.'

'Well – you haven't any aspirin, have you?'

'No. Sorry.'

He went out.

I heaved a sigh and threw myself on the bed. So this was the way it was. Would there always be this same prickly fear, this same sinking at the stomach?

I looked at the clock. I thought of Bannister lying dead. I shuddered. Yes, it must be all over by now. Soon the police—

Suddenly I remembered the bloodstains in the car, what I must do, and quickly.

I hurried down to the car and filled a bucket of water. Then I took a sponge and started washing away the stains. I was careful not to do too good a job, just good enough to make it seem that I was trying to cover up.

I tried not to think of Bannister being killed, but the blood kept me from thinking of anything else. I saw him falling, his twisted leg bent under him, his eyes looking wonderstruck at Grisby and the gun as he fell . . .

I heard footsteps crunching on gravel. The sound stopped. I waited, holding my breath. Silence . . . maybe I had imagined it, then . . .

Something made me look up at the window.

My hair stood on end.

Framed in the window was the face of Elsa Bannister.

Her mouth was open in surprise. She seemed white – frightened.

I dropped the sponge and went out to her.

'I was out for a walk,' she said, 'I saw the light, and your shadow moving. I came over to see what was wrong.'

'Why, nothing,' I said. 'A little accident. I ran into a truck—'

'You're hurt!' She looked at the cuts on my face, in the light from the window. Her hands went up to my face.

'It isn't anything. Just a few scratches.'

She was in my arms, trembling, holding me tight. Her lips quiv-

ered at my kiss. Then she drew back. There was something on her
mind.

'Laurence—'

'Yes?'

'You said last night . . . you said that you wanted to go back to sea.'

I waited, surprised.

'I just wanted to tell you – if you still think you ought to go—'

I felt as though I had been struck. If she hadn't stopped me last
night I would have been gone. I wouldn't have had this terrible weight
hanging over me, this feeling of guilt and of terror.

For the first time, too, it came to me that now she was a widow. A
widow!

'You mean that you *want* me to go?' I asked.

'I mean that I want you to be happy.'

She was very earnest. She spoke slowly, thinking over each word.

'You see, I know how it is to feel caught – to be forced to stay in
one place. I have been married for eight years. For eight years I have
been – a prisoner.'

When she said 'prisoner,' I jumped. Did she know? But that was
impossible!

She went on: 'So I know how you feel about going back to sea.
Why not go – now, *tonight*?'

I couldn't believe it.

'You *want* me to go?' I asked again.

She caught her lower lip with her teeth. Her eyes filled with tears.
She drew the back of her hand across her face.

'No,' she said.

I held her in my arms. Her body grew limp. Her hair became loose
and tumbled down over my hands in cool waves. We kissed. My blood
sang, 'Now, now!'

I carried her to the house and over the threshold.

There was a light on in one room. It threw a soft orange glow over
a lounge in the corner.

As I lowered her, her arms tightened. Her kiss rocked me on my
feet.

Now, now! . . .

A cough came behind us.

I jumped back.

My heart pounded.

It was Broome again. He came into the light, lurching a little to one side. Then he saw us.

'Oh—' he said.

He started to back out.

Mrs Bannister was on her feet. She seemed very cool.

'What is it, Broome?'

Broome came back into the light. He looked from one to the other of us, smirking.

'You've been drinking . . . I'm afraid I will have to speak to Mr Bannister about you.'

Broome shook his head. He explained: 'I knocked and no one answered. I thought you were out. I've been trying to find an aspirin. My head's killing me.'

He must have come into the house while we were talking outside the garage. It was strange we hadn't heard him. But everything was strange about this night.

She hesitated, looking at him.

'Oh, I see. There's some upstairs in the cabinet. The maid – or wait – I suppose I'll have to get them for you.'

She went out, frowning and fixing her hair.

Broome winked at me. He pursed his lips into a whistle.

'You're pretty good,' he said.

'What do you mean?'

'You know what I mean. Pretending she couldn't be touched with a ten-foot pole – all that gaff you handed me about her. You had me fooled, too, for a while.'

'You're crazy,' I said. 'You're imagining things. She wouldn't look at me any more than she would at you. Why—'

'I suppose you're going to tell me you weren't kissing her just now.'

'Why, you—'

I would like to have smashed his face in as he stood there leering. But I knew he was drunk and not responsible.

'Well, weren't you? Understand, I take my hat off—'

He didn't really see us, then. He was leaping at conclusions just from finding me there with her. That was better. If he had seen us, he might have thought, when he heard of Bannister being killed, that she and I had planned it together.

'You're crazy,' I said again.

'Then what are you doing here?'

'She noticed the car was smashed when I drove it into the garage. She wanted to hear all about the accident. I told her.'

He was disappointed.

When Mrs Bannister came back into the room, he was respectful again.

'I hope you will feel better now,' she said.

He thanked her and went out.

When he had gone, we looked at each other. We both felt cheated.

'Do you suppose he saw us?' she whispered tensely.

'No, I know he didn't. I could tell by what he said. You needn't worry.'

'I wasn't worrying about myself, but about you. Marco – Mr Bannister – is insanely jealous. You might as well know. He might even try to kill you if he learned—'

I took her in my arms again. Suddenly I thought that maybe everything would be all right, after all.

But her kiss had fear in it.

'No, please. You'll have to go. Broome will notice if you stay too long.'

'He's too drunk to notice anything.'

She shook her head, biting her lip.

'I'm afraid he was only pretending. I think he saw us come in together, and used that for an excuse. I told you that Mr Bannister was jealous. I think he hired Broome to watch—'

'He hired Broome!'

'Why, yes, of course.'

'But Broome told me you hired him. He said you saw him at the Innes place and told him to drop over here after he'd finished. He said you liked the work he was doing for them.'

Her mouth opened in surprise.

'You mean that isn't true?' I asked.

She clutched my arm. She seemed really frightened now.

'No. Not one word of it is true! Did he ask you questions about me? Did he try to draw you out at all or become friends with you?'

'He asked me if there wasn't someone you met in town, when I drove you in, or if anyone came out here to see you. I told him he had you all wrong. He doesn't know about us, but he guesses. He's suspicious of everyone, even Grisby.'

'Then that proves it.' Her hand on my arm tightened. 'He's no more a gardener than you or I. He's a detective!'

IV

Through the wall I could hear Broome snoring.

I couldn't sleep myself.

Why didn't they come?

The clock ticked on. It was after two; still they did not come.

Except for Broome's drunken sleeping, everything was still. Not a sound came from the house. But there was a light on in Elsa's room. Now and then a shadow passed the window. I could feel her near, and was glad.

The light went out. Now I was alone.

I walked back and forth, back and forth. Not even the chirping of a cricket. Yet there was a tightening at the throat – as though everything was closing in on me.

Suddenly I knew I was not going to go through with it. Grisby was a fool to think I would. How did I know it wasn't all a trick of his to fasten Bannister's killing on me and protect himself?

Five thousand dollars was cheap for having someone go to the chair for you.

I had it! Grisby had never had any thought of going away. He'd paid me the five thousand so he wouldn't have to go! And there I was, walking right into the electric chair for him, just as he was counting on me doing.

What if he had threatened to come back and get me if I didn't go through with it? I would be at sea by the time he knew.

I started for the door, switching out the light.

The glare of headlights turning into the drive came through the window. For a minute it blinded me.

Brakes screeched. Motorcycle stands clicked into place. Car doors banged. There was the sound of many men walking on gravel.

The night was suddenly alive with voices.

'Cover the house. We'll try the garage.'

I heard the garage door open and men moving below.

'McCracken!' one said. 'Look at this!'

'Find something?'

'Look at the car – it's smashed. He must have hit something getting away.'

'What's this, on the seat here?'

'Blood!'

'We got him, all right.'

There was a moment's stunned silence, and then:

'Maybe he's taken a run-out powder.'

A man laughed hoarsely.

'What would he be bringing the car back for, then? No, he's here, all right.'

'Come on – let's get him!'

I slipped out of the room and down the dark hall to the rear. There was a window here. It was open.

Broome's bed creaked. He had heard the voices. He knew the police were after me.

His light flashed on.

He saw me at the window. He lurched forward.

Men were starting up the stairs.

I struck out. The blow hit Broome squarely. He reeled back and then crashed forward to the floor.

I scrambled through the window. For a second I hung on the ledge. Then I dropped.

There were bushes here. I went in and out of them, running bent over, gasping, stumbling, falling.

A shout went up behind me.

'Quick – get him! He just went out the window!'

I ran on. I reached the hedge that lined the drive. I followed it to the road.

Motorcycles started up. They were going to head me off!

I crossed the road and plunged into the woods on the other side. It was so dark I couldn't see. I felt my way along. My lungs were bursting. Branches scratched me. I hit a stump. I fell. I lay panting.

Suddenly moonlight soaked through the trees. I could see now. I went on. The voices of men beating the woods followed me.

The woods broke. Underfoot the ground became soft, soggy.

I stopped and listened.

The motorcycles were roaring up and down the road. Sirens screamed. Scattered voices issued from the woods. Flashlights stabbed the darkness. They were coming closer.

I saw that where I had come out of the woods was the edge of the swamp. The weeds here were waist high. Low over the swamp to the east a great round moon had broken through the clouds. It gave a ghostly glow to the haze. In the west, the sky was still torn with rolling sheets of lightning. A rumbling came from the west.

I ran bent over through the weeds. Soon there was water. I splashed through it knee-deep. I came on to drier ground.

Suddenly the ruins of an old building loomed up ahead. The front half of the building was gone. The jagged sides and the rear rose up and were lost in the writhing wisps of the haze.

I climbed over fallen beams and went in.

It was dark inside. I moved toward the back, toward shafts of moonlight pouring through a window onto stairs. Tiny bright eyes glinted from the stairs.

The voices seemed very near. The police had entered the swamp!

I went forward to the stairs. At the first creak, a horde of rats moved out from underneath. There was a sudden rush, then silence as they watched me climb.

A step broke. I leaped clear.

Now I was at the top. Part of the floor remained. There was a dark corner where the roof still stood. I climbed on hands and knees. Boards caved under me and crashed to the floor below. I reached the corner. I lay still, panting and shaking.

Soon the rats began to come. They squatted around in a circle, watching. The moonlight shone on their glossy coats. Their tails were thick and long. They looked as big and fat as tomcats. They sat and waited.

I took a stick and threw it at them. They scampered. In a minute they were back. They sat and waited.

A boiling hatred of rats mounted in me. They seemed so smug and superior. I would like to have killed them all.

As though they read my thoughts, they turned and ran.

My breathing came easier now. I stood up and looked over the edge of the ruins.

Now I could see why the rats had run. Men were coming. They were closing in upon the old building from three sides. Their flashlights ripped the haze.

I lay down and did not move.

Voices came up to me as the men met below.

'Try the stairs,' someone said.

Another: 'Watch it! He may have a gun!'

The rats were very still.

The stairs creaked. Now the rats scurried from all directions. They raced under the feet of the men moving up the stairs.

'He couldn't have gone up here. There's a big gap where the stairs have caved in.'

'Well, he's in one of these buildings.'

A voice boomed: 'Jesus, a rat! Right under my feet. I must have stepped on him. He was big as a house.'

The men went out.

Slowly the voices died away.

I looked up. The tiny bright eyes were glinting at me again. I threw another stick. The rats were tired of the game. They scarcely budged.

I was worn out with shock and terror and physical exhaustion. I wanted only to sleep. That was impossible. I remembered reading of a man who was sleeping with his hand dangling over the bed to the floor. When he woke up half his hand was chewed away. And he hadn't felt a thing.

There was another reason, too, why I couldn't sleep. Now that the police were looking for me, the whole thing took on a reality it had not had before. For the first time the horror of what I had done came to me. A sort of delirium possessed me, in which Bannister appeared . . .

Suddenly I saw him.

He was coming toward me!

In his hand was a gnarled cane. He walked with his usual comic swing. The haze curled around him. He came straight toward the building, the clump-clump of his feet ringing on the hard ground.

The rats did not move. They did not hear him. Then he wasn't real. But I could hear him and I could see him coming through the haze. I could see him very clearly. I could see him come to the edge of the building and stand leaning on his cane. I could see him looking – looking up at me!

I crouched back.

There was a rat in the corner with me. It squealed as I pressed against it.

I could stand it no longer; I jumped up. I leaped down the stairs, far out over the broken part, and raced toward the front of the building.

Bannister saw me coming. He raised his cane to strike.

I stopped dead with fright, my heart pounding.

All the horror and terror I had known was as nothing compared to this moment.

We stood looking at each other, he with the cane still raised, me panting, half paralyzed.

Slowly I backed away from him, back into the ruins. Once in darkness, I darted through a window at the rear and plunged through the weeds into the swamp. No one followed me. Yet it felt as though ghosts were on every side, clinging, holding me back. Wraithlike forms loomed up ahead.

I tried to go faster. My feet sank to the knees in mud and slime. Rats scurried and squealed beneath.

I reached the woods. I raced headlong to the road. I wanted to hear voices again, to feel people near me.

A spotlight was covering the road. Voices came from the house and garage.

I entered the spotlight. I walked up the path of light to the cars.

A policeman came out through the door of the garage. He gaped at me.

I went straight up to him. I almost collapsed at his feet.

'I'm the one they're looking for,' I said. I could hardly talk. 'I want to – to give myself up!'

V

They had me in the center of the room – my room, up above the garage. They were all talking to me at once, waiting for the others to come back. They leaned over me and shouted.

'Why did you kill him?'

'Come on – spill it!'

'Better talk, kid – you'll save yourself a lot of grief.'

The room was torn apart. The mattress was half off the bed. Books were scattered around the room. The duffle bag was out in the middle. Everything in it had been dumped onto the floor.

A big man in plain-clothes came through the door – Sergeant McCracken.

'So you gave yourself up,' he said. 'That was the smart thing to do, all right.'

A policeman took a cap out from inside his coat and put it on my head. He yanked the brim down over my eyes, tight.

'Is that yours?' he demanded.

I worked the cap loose and looked at it.

'Yes,' I said. 'Why?'

'Why!' he yelled.

He slammed me down into the chair. He was a tall thin man with a long nose. Dance was his name. He poked the nose into my face.

'All right!' he shouted. 'That cap was found beside the body. Now are you going to talk, or must I ram it down your throat?'

I gulped.

'What would I be killing anyone for?' I asked.

'That's what you're going to tell us.'

McCracken took the packet of bills out of his pocket. The blood-stains on it looked bigger than ever.

'Here's why,' he said. 'We found these stuffed into the mattress. Five thousand dollars! You might as well tell us about it. I can tell to look at you that you're not a killer. What happened?'

I was so tired and bruised, I was willing to say anything if they would only let me alone. I saw now that of course I had to tell them about Grisby. It was my only chance.

I said: 'First I want to know where you found this cap.'

'Sure, sure. As if you didn't know. At the foot of Wall Street, just where you left it.'

I looked surprised.

'But I couldn't have left it there!'

'The hell you couldn't. You did.'

The tall man cuffed me on the cheek. He thrust his nose into my face again.

'Are you going to talk, or aren't you?'

'Listen!' I said. 'I wasn't down at Wall Street tonight. I was down at the beach.'

'Sure you were,' he said. 'You were having a nice cool dip for yourself. We know it. But will the judge believe it? That's what's worrying us.'

'What did you run away for if you didn't do it?' McCracken asked. He was the nicest one of the lot. I decided not to pay any attention to the others, but to talk to him.

'Mr Grisby came out about ten o'clock,' I told him. 'I drove him down to the station, when he'd got what he came for here. We missed the train. It was hot. He suggested that we drive down to the beach while we waited for the next train. On the way we had an accident. We ran into a truck. The name of the truck driver is Steve Crunch.'

'You're taking all this down?' McCracken asked a policeman.

I saw that the policeman had a notebook and was taking it all down.

I went on: 'Down at the beach where we parked the car we thought we heard a sound. Grisby said maybe it was a stick-up. I took the gun out of the side-pocket of the car, and just then the gun went off. I hadn't meant it to. The bullet hit Grisby and I saw that he was dead. I got panicky. Even though it was an accident, it might look like murder. So I weighted the body down and threw it in the Sound. He couldn't be any deader, and that way I thought I would be safe.'

'Were you wearing your cap?'

'Oh, yes. I don't know how I lost it, but I was pretty excited. People were on the beach, all up and down, and they heard the shot. They came up running. When they got there I was alone, of course. They decided everything was all right. So I came on back here.'

'What time did you get back?'

He wouldn't believe it if I told him about the lights of the car going out and holding me up for half an hour. Nobody saw me coming back.

'It was eleven o'clock,' I said. 'I know, because I looked at the clock.'

'And then you tried to wash the bloodstains from the car.'

'Naturally. It was just an accident, and I didn't want to get in any trouble because of it. Even if I went free, I might lose my job. It was the only one I'd been able to get in a year.'

'You were broke when you took the job?'

'I didn't have a cent.'

'And how long have you been here?'

'About eight weeks.'

'Did you like it here?'

'Yes, I liked it fine.'

'Mrs Bannister says you were all set to leave last night, that you wanted to go back to sea.'

She must have said that to defend me, to show that I couldn't have had any premeditated ideas of murder. Now it looked like it was going to act as a boomerang.

'I was thinking of going, yes.'

'I guess you weren't satisfied with the money you were making here?'

'What do you mean?'

McCracken tapped the five thousand dollars.

'You think I got that from Grisby?' I asked.

'We're asking you.'

The tall man pushed me in the back of the head.

'I suppose he's going to tell us he got it from singing in opera,' he said.

'I found it,' I said.

'Sure you found it. You found it right down at the foot of Wall Street, where all the money comes from. J. P. Morgan must have dropped it. He wouldn't know the difference, a piking five thousand.'

'All right,' I said. 'I got it off of Grisby. I didn't want anyone identifying him if he ever bobbed up and I took all his things out of his pockets. I burned the rest, but I didn't burn that. Why should I? It wasn't any good to him any more.'

They asked a lot of other questions. I was confused, but I remembered clearly that the main thing I had to do was prove that I couldn't have been off murdering someone else as long as I was killing Grisby and throwing his body in the Sound. I told about Mrs Bannister asking about the car and the accident when I got home. And I repeated the time – about eleven o'clock. I knew I must stick to that, whatever happened.

'You can prove that?' McCracken asked.

I did some fast thinking. I remembered that Broome was drunk; he wouldn't have known whether it had been eleven or eleven-thirty.

'Sure,' I said. 'Ask Broome, he'll tell you.'

Dance laughed.

'That's a good one,' he said. 'For two cents I'd—'

'Never mind that now,' McCracken said. He handed me the notebook. 'Just sign what you've said here and we'll take the rest of it up when we get you down to headquarters.'

I played the part very well. It was just as Grisby said, anything to get out of the Bannister killing.

But my hand shook as I signed the paper.

'That's fine,' said McCracken.

He took the confession, the cap, and the money and put them inside his coat.

'And now suppose you tell us how you happened to kill Broome,' he said.

VI

'Broome!'

I remembered hitting him when he tried to stop me from going out the window. But I couldn't have killed him with the blow – I couldn't have! It wouldn't even have knocked him out, if he hadn't been drunk.

McCracken narrowed his eyes.

'You're not going to pretend you didn't know?'

'You mean he's really dead – *Broome?*'

'Oh, he's dead, all right.'

'But how – he *couldn't* be dead!'

'Look here. You didn't give us any trouble about Grisby. Why hold out on this? You probably found out he was a detective. Maybe he called you on the bloodstains in the car, or on your clothes. Whatever it was, you knew you wouldn't be safe unless you got him out of the way. Maybe everything you said about Grisby and the accident is true. But accident or not, you admit you tried to cover up by weighting the body and throwing it in the Sound. What good would all that be if Broome found out?'

'It wouldn't be any good, but if he'd found out, I would have told him the truth. I did with you, didn't I?'

'Then you're going to stand by the Grisby confession, but balk on the Broome angle?'

'I didn't kill Broome!' I said. 'Why should I tell you I did?'

Dance came up beside me and doubled up a bony fist. He looked at McCracken.

'Shall I try the lie-detector on him?'

He waved the fist in front of my face.

'No. He'll talk.'

'How was he killed?' I asked.

'He was choked to death.'

Then it couldn't have been the blow that did it. But who would choke him, and why? My head was in a whirl.

'Where did you find him?' I asked.

McCracken jerked his head toward Broome's room.

'In there,' he said. 'On the floor. Fully dressed, but he'd been lying down on the bed.'

'Well, I didn't do it.'

'Any idea who did?'

'No. He was all right when I went out the window, because I saw him. So it must have happened after you'd got here.'

'You mean he saw you go out the window, and didn't try to stop you?'

'He did try. That was when you were coming up the steps. He came for me and I hit him. I'll admit that. But there wasn't time for me to have choked him, even if I'd wanted to.'

'Unless you did it before we came.'

'I didn't, though!'

McCracken looked sad.

'Well, you'd better think fast about who did do it, then, because everything points to you. Did you know he was a detective?'

'Uh—'

'You did, didn't you?'

'I guessed he was. I didn't know.'

'But you weren't taking any chances.'

'I told you, I didn't do it.'

McCracken turned abruptly and started for the door.

'Come with me,' he said.

I followed him into the next room. He watched my every move, my every expression, all the while we were there. I felt as guilty as though I had really killed Broome and was trying to cover up. I knew that he sensed this guilt, and that the others in the room sensed it.

Broome was lying on his back with one hand to his throat. His face was black, and his tongue, swollen, protruded from blue lips. There was no sign of a struggle.

McCracken said nothing. The rest of the men said nothing. All looked at me.

'You're sure he was choked?'

'Look at those bruises on his throat. And look at the way his tie is twisted – that's how he was choked!'

I looked. I wet my lips. My own tongue felt swollen. It seemed that the hands that were at his throat were at mine.

'You still don't want to talk?'

I gulped.

'I don't understand it,' I said.

'You mean if you didn't do it, who else *could* have, don't you?'

'Yes.'

'That's my point. If you didn't, who else could have? You'd better talk, kid – for your own sake. But you don't have to.'

We went back to my room. I slumped down into a chair.

'Get your things ready,' said McCracken. 'You'll be gone a long time.'

Elsa came in. She was wearing a bathrobe over her negligee – Bannister's white robe with the cowl hanging loose. She came up to me and put a hand on my shoulder.

'Laurence—' she said.

I felt like crying when I looked at her. Her eyes were half filled with tears.

'Yes'm?'

'Laurence, did you really do this thing?'

I didn't know whether she was talking about Bannister, Grisby or Broome.

I bowed my head. I would like to have gotten her alone and told her about it, how I was caught in it against my will, how I would have run out if she hadn't stopped me the way she did. I couldn't talk to her here, however. I said nothing.

'But how could you?' she asked. 'Oh, I'm sure he couldn't have,' she said to McCracken.

He shook his head.

'You never can tell by the looks of people what they'll do. One question I'd like to ask you, though, Mrs Bannister. He says he was back here by eleven o'clock and that you asked him about the car being smashed. Can you be sure about the time?'

I caught my breath and waited, sweating.

'Yes, I know he was back before eleven.'

I let out breath.

'How can you be sure?' McCracken asked her.

'Broome came in asking for an aspirin. While I was getting it I noticed the time. It was a few minutes after eleven and he had been back about ten minutes then.'

I looked at her. From the way she talked, it sounded as though she really thought I was back before eleven. It sounded, too, as though she thought Broome was still alive.

'And what time was it that Grisby left?' McCracken went on.

She thought a minute before answering. She looked very beautiful.

'Why, I don't really know. I was downtown shopping and had stopped for a show. He had left by the time I returned.'

'What time was that?'

'That was about ten-thirty, so he must have come before then. The maid must have let him in—'

'Yes, we've talked to her. She said he got here at ten.'

'But, then – she must have told you I wasn't here when he came!'

'Oh, she did. But she said she went to sleep right after he left. We have to check every detail – sorry. And now, I think, if you want to get some sleep—'

She went out looking back over her shoulder at me. I knew she would have liked to stay and help me still more, but she couldn't let on that there was anything between us.

I hauled out the duffle bag and got ready to leave.

And then my heart somersaulted.

Someone was coming up the stairs.

My blood chilled. I was paralyzed. I couldn't move or take my eyes from the door. And suddenly, there he was—

BANNISTER!

He came clumping into the room. My mouth hung open. I forced my eyes down to his feet. His shoes were covered with mud. His cane was tipped with clay.

Then he WAS *in the swamp! It* WAS *he in the moonlight, looking up at me! It* WAS *he who raised his cane to strike!*

I heard his voice.

'So they found you!' he said.

His cane tapped me on the arm. I sprang back and away from him. My hand went to my mouth to stop the scream on my lips.

HE WASN'T DEAD. SOMETHING HAD GONE WRONG.

My head felt like it would crack. The whole truth crashed in on me.

IT WAS GRISBY WHO WAS DEAD.

IT WAS GRISBY WHO LAY BLEEDING DOWN ON WALL STREET.

AND I HAD JUST CONFESSED TO KILLING HIM!

PART THREE

I

There was plenty of time to figure out what must have happened –
plenty.

They took me down to the old Homicide Court on Mott Street
for what they called the arraignment. I was held without bail 'pending
action Grand Jury.' Then they took me to the Tombs. That's where
the Bridge of Sighs is. The bridge goes over to the Criminal Courts
building, where they try you. 'Guilty' or 'Not guilty' – that's where
you get the news.

Because I'd signed the confession – and wasn't *that* a smart thing
to do; I had Grisby to thank for that – they had nothing else to do but
hold me for the trial.

While you wait you can play solitaire, or read a book, or see what
the papers are saying about you.

The papers were all saying the confession I'd made was phony.
How could I have killed Grisby out on Bannister's beach, on Long
Island, and have his body turn up at the foot of Wall Street? It might
have been an accident, my killing him, but if I had thrown him in the
Sound, as I said in the confession, how could he turn up on Wall Street
with his clothes dry?

Not that they didn't believe I'd killed him – or Broome, either. It
was just that they couldn't figure it out. They'd found witnesses who
had seen me on the beach, and who had heard the shot. All said I'd
been alone when they saw me. So they figured I must have gone down
to the beach *after* killing Grisby on Wall Street, and then tried to make
it look as though I had killed him on the beach, accidentally, as I'd said.

But then Steve Crunch, the truck driver, told how I had run into
him with Bannister's car – he had the license number and everything,

even Grisby's card – and swore up and down that the man with me had been Grisby. He described him. He told about the cut on Grisby's wrist. Sure enough, when they went to look, there was the cut, just as Crunch had said.

Well, then! Since that was only a little while before the shot on the beach, when people had come running and had found me alone, how could I have got rid of his body unless I *had* thrown it into the Sound? People had seen me coming up from the pier, too – it all checked with my confession.

And the money they'd found in my room had been traced to Grisby's bank – he'd withdrawn it just that day – and I had seen him take it out! That had been one of Grisby's bright ideas, too, that I should go with him – just to make sure I'd get the money when I'd done my job. Yes! Just to make sure that the police would believe I had killed him – I saw that now!

But the main thing was, if Mrs Bannister had been right about the time that she saw me back in the garage, I *couldn't* have taken Grisby – or his body – down to the foot of Wall Street.

So there was the mystery that puzzled the papers – not who had killed Grisby (they'd even found my *cap* clutched in his hand) but how I had managed the thing.

You'd think they'd got it into their heads, finally, that maybe someone else had killed him. They didn't. They couldn't see how I had killed him, maybe, but every clue pointed to me (just as it was meant to do, in Grisby's 'perfect crime'). Besides, what would I confess for if I *hadn't* killed him? The police hadn't given me any third degree. McCracken knew that, even if nobody else did. I had confessed of my own free will.

Of course, I *hadn't* confessed to killing Broome. Yet it was a cinch that Broome was killed to prevent his talking – the two crimes were tied up together. And I had confessed to killing Grisby, hadn't I?

Well, the papers had the explanation for that, too. A jury might agree I had killed Grisby accidentally, as I said. But it never could agree that Broome had been *choked* accidentally. So of course I hadn't confessed to that.

Not that anyone cared, even the District Attorney. With all the evidence against me, especially my seeing Grisby draw the money out of the bank, they felt sure they could laugh any 'accident' plea right out of court.

But they knew they'd have to have some reasonable explanation, too, of how I could kill Grisby out on Bannister's beach, throw the body in the Sound there, and then have it come up *dry* at the foot of Wall Street!

McCracken came into my cell the second day to get the answer to that.

'That was pretty clever, all right,' he said. 'I'll have to hand it to you. But how'd you manage it? That's what I'd like to know.'

'I didn't manage it,' I said. 'How could I?'

'You still insist you threw the body in the Sound?'

'Yes.' I had in mind taking back the whole confession, but I had to figure it all out first. If I told what really had happened, they might just laugh at me. Besides, I wasn't sure yet whether I ought to tell about how Grisby had planned to kill Bannister, because that might let me in for it, too, even if I got out of this.

'Well, then,' said McCracken, 'if you still insist you threw the body in the Sound, how do you explain that Grisby's clothes were dry when we picked him up at Wall Street?'

'I can't explain it.'

'He couldn't have floated there.'

'No, I guess not.'

He offered me a cigarette. We sat and smoked. All the while he looked at me.

'You're a cool one, all right,' he said. 'But about this – this mystery, as the papers call it. How could Grisby have got down there, after you shot him on the beach? He was seen with you, just a little while before. That truck driver – Crunch is his name, you told us about him your-self – he saw you with Grisby.'

'Sure he did. I told you.'

'Well, then, how could Grisby get down to Wall Street? It was just an hour after Crunch saw you with him that we found Grisby dead *down on Wall Street*. How could you get him there?'

'I don't know.'

'Well, then, I'll tell you. You took him down there in a boat – a speedboat!'

'I didn't! In the first place, I wouldn't have had time. I went right to the garage from the beach. Ask Mrs Bannister. Could I have got down there and *back*, even in a speedboat, before eleven o'clock?'

'No, you couldn't – unless you got Mrs Bannister to lie about the time you were back at the house.'

So that was it!

'I didn't!' I said. 'She'd have no reason to lie for me, anyway – why should she?'

'All right, then. If you didn't take him down there, who did? He couldn't have taken himself down!'

'Why not?' My voice was shaking.

'Why not?' he said. 'Because there was no way for him to get down. He didn't take the train; we checked that. He didn't drive, or we'd have found the car. And he didn't take the speedboat, because how could he have got it back?'

'Back! Back where?'

'Why, back at Bannister's beach, where you bumped him!'

'Back at Bannister's beach!'

'Sure. Why not?'

'But – Why, it *couldn't* be!'

I began to tremble all over. Something was wrong somewhere. That boat *couldn't* have got back by itself – unless by Grisby's ghost!

'You mean it wasn't there when you were with him?' he asked.

Chills raced up and down my spine.

'Oh, it was there, all right—'

'Well, then, what was to stop you from taking him down in the boat and then coming back that way yourself?'

'I told you, there wouldn't have been time!'

'All right, then – either you had someone working with you or he took himself down and the boat just drifted back.'

I changed the subject.

'What would he go down to Wall Street for?'

'People who are shot do funny things sometimes. Or maybe he didn't think the wound was serious, or at least as serious as it was, and that he'd have a doctor come up and fix it at the office. Remember, he was due there. That would be as good a place as any to have it looked over, and easy to get to in the boat. The office is only half a block from the river. It looks like he got out of the boat and started for the office, but couldn't make it.'

'Maybe he'd already been to the office and was *coming back* to the boat when he died.'

He shook his head.

'The night watchman would have seen him. He checks everyone in and out at that hour.'

'Maybe he went in and out the back way. Would the watchman have seen him then?'

'No, but the back door was locked from the inside – he couldn't have come in that way. Besides, the position of the body shows that he was coming toward the building, not going away. No, if you're going to try to squeeze out of this, you'll have to find a better angle than that. What you're trying to do is show that someone else might have killed him, isn't that it?'

'All I mean is that my shot might only have stunned him, and that he would have been all right if someone else hadn't shot him down there.'

'Well, you can forget about that, then. He was only shot once – and at close range.'

'Who found the body down there – Bannister?'

'No. The copper on the beat found him. He recognized him and told the night watchman in Grisby's building. The watchman called Bannister, and they went out to make sure it was Grisby. It was, all right . . . and with your cap in his hand.'

'Well, but if Grisby took himself down there, that lets me out, doesn't it?'

'Why? It was still your shot that killed him. The only out you have – maybe – is that you shot him accidentally. I'm just trying to figure out how the whole thing could have happened.'

Just then a man came in. He was short, with a bumpy red face and bright black eyes.

'Oh, hello, Meade,' said McCracken. 'Got the report yet on that Grisby bullet?'

'Yep. And the bullet that killed Grisby doesn't check with the gun the kid here had.'

'It doesn't! You mean the gun that was found in the car?'

'That's right.' He turned and looked at me. 'Now, you – what'd you do with the gun you used, throw it in the Sound?'

'No,' I said. 'That was the only gun I had.'

'Sure,' said McCracken. 'It had his fingerprints on it – and one shell had just been fired! How about that?'

'Don't ask me,' said Meade. 'I'm just telling you.'

II

It was a mix-up, all right. The only thing was, I was the most mixed up of all.

I said I had plenty of time to figure it out. I did. But that's all the good it did me.

The way I figured it, Bannister had found out about the plan to kill him. He'd been suspecting something like that to happen, otherwise why had he put Broome out there to watch? Well, Broome had been snooping around, probably, and had found the note I'd written to Bannister. You know, the note telling about Grisby's perfect crime, and which I'd later torn up. He'd told Bannister, of course. And Bannister, knowing all suspicion was to be thrown on me, had let Grisby go ahead – up to the point of the murder. Then he'd turned the tables. He'd got Grisby first.

That was the way I figured it. It was the only way I *could* figure it.

There was only one thing wrong with the picture. Bannister had been waiting for Grisby in their offices. The night watchman, who checked everyone in and out of the building, said (according to the papers) that Bannister hadn't gone out. Then how could he have shot Grisby? Had he fired at him from a window? It would have had to be some shot – half a block in dim light.

Anyway, that's not what happened. It couldn't have been. McCracken said Grisby had been shot at close range. And the bullet had entered just about like it would have if I *had* fired with him sitting next to me in the car.

And what about Broome?

Of course, if Broome had seen the note I'd written and had told Bannister of the plan, and if Bannister had then killed Grisby, he'd naturally want to be sure Broome didn't talk. Because Broome would be the only one, then, who would know of his motive for killing Grisby – outside of me, that is. With Broome out of the way, the police wouldn't know of the motive . . . not unless I told them.

Well, why couldn't I tell them?

Bannister would have had that all figured out, just as I was figuring it out now. He'd know I wouldn't dare tell the truth. It would be too damaging. I'd have to admit my part in the scheme to kill Bannister. And how would it help me to prove I didn't kill Grisby by admitting that I was trying to help Grisby kill Bannister? If I would do that for money, why wouldn't I kill Grisby for money – supposing I could get more that way? And they'd say that's just what happened, and show the five thousand to prove it. They wouldn't believe it if I said that Grisby had threatened to kill me if I didn't go through with it.

Not only that, but what was my word against Bannister's? I was just a chauffeur – and maybe sore at Bannister, to boot. I'd started to leave my job, hadn't I? Besides, I was fighting for my life. Naturally I'd try to pin the murder on someone else.

The third day I was in jail the guard came and told me someone wanted to see me. He led me to a room with tables divided by a screen.

'Five minutes,' he said.

I sat down at a table and looked across at Elsa Bannister. She was wearing a black dress low at the neck, a black hat, and a veil down to the tip of her nose.

'I would have come before,' she said breathlessly. 'I couldn't.'

She looked pale and worried, but still very beautiful.

For a minute we just looked into each other's eyes.

I felt weak, and at the same time so strong I could have torn the screen open to get at her, if she'd asked me.

Her lips twitched into the sad-sweet smile that always made me want to crush them – hard.

'I'm glad you came,' I said. The guard was listening.

'I had to see you,' she whispered. 'I shouldn't have come, even now. I had to.'

'You mean that Bannister knows about us?'

'No; but he mustn't. It would spoil everything.'

I looked at the guard. He wasn't much interested. He was chewing one end of a mouse-colored moustache.

'What are you going to do?' she asked.

'Why, nothing.'

'But the confession—'

'Oh, that. If I have to, I'll just take it back. You didn't believe it, did you?'

'I knew if you had done it, it must have been an accident, just as you said it was.'

'Well,' I said, 'it wasn't an accident. And I didn't do it.'

'I know,' she said. 'But I'm glad to hear you say it.'

'Who do you think *did* do it?'

'I'm afraid to think.'

'Bannister?'

She caught her breath and looked up at the guard.

'I shouldn't have said that, maybe,' I whispered, 'but I can't see who else could have done it. Can you?'

'I don't know. I'm afraid, Laurence – I only know we mustn't let them find you guilty. You'll have to have a lawyer.'

'I haven't any money for a lawyer.'

'I know. But you won't need any, Laurence—'

'Yes?'

'I shouldn't have come here.' She leaned forward and whispered intensely, 'If my husband knew, he'd refuse to help you.'

'Help me!'

'Yes. He has quite made up his mind to it.'

'But he's the one I think—'

'I know. But, Laurence, whatever else you say – whatever anyone says – he is one of the best criminal lawyers in New York county. He's never lost a big case – never!'

I shook my head.

'The State has lawyers,' I said. 'They'll give me one. If I'd really killed anyone, it might be different.'

She leaned forward, frowning.

'Laurence, you've got to listen to me. We can't take any chances. Everyone believes you're guilty – you even signed a confession. You need the best defense counsel you can get. What if Marco did – what if he is responsible for Mr Grisby's murder? Then he would *know* you weren't guilty! That would be all the more reason for wanting to save you, wouldn't it?'

I thought that over, but there was something about it that didn't strike just right. If he knew I'd been in this thing against him, with Grisby, what would he want to help me get off for? He wouldn't. He'd want to see me go to the chair. Even if he'd killed Grisby himself. He'd want to get both of us.

'After all,' she said, 'you worked for him. Naturally, he'd want to help you, if only for the looks of the thing.'

'Does he think I did it?'

'I don't know. He says he doesn't think you're the type to have done it. He prides himself on being able to read character. Anyway, he really wants to take the case—'

'I'll bet you put that idea into his head.'

'Oh, no – really. It was his own idea, entirely. I *do* think it's a real break for you. I came down to make sure you would accept. I thought that maybe you might believe he had done it, and would refuse.'

'That's just what I do think.'

'But you must let him help you, don't you see? Please, Laurence – for my sake – won't you?'

'Well,' I said, 'I'll know better what to say after I talk to him.'

We looked at each other until the screen between us seemed to vibrate. Then her eyes clouded over and tears came into them. She put a handkerchief inside her veil. The perfume started my head reeling.

'I can't lose you now,' she said.

My eyes began to smart. She seemed to fade away in a blur.

'I'll be out soon, don't you worry,' I said. And that's the first time I thought maybe I wouldn't.

'I do worry. Laurence, you have to accept his help. It may be your only chance. Promise me!'

'All right,' I said.

'Good!' She put her handkerchief back into her bag. 'I'll have to hurry now – I can't have him finding me here. You know how jealous he is. But I'll be back.'

The guard came over and tapped me on the shoulder.

'Five minutes,' he said.

Elsa stood up.

'Soon,' I said.

'Yes.'

I watched her going out, her head held down. Her black dress rippled sleekly as she walked.

The door clanged shut.

III

That society woman who shot her husband (five times) while he was raiding the icebox for a midnight snack came up for trial while I was in the jail.

I saw her picture in the paper. She was a beauty, all right. You couldn't imagine her killing her husband on purpose.

The State had built up a strong case against her, though. They had witnesses to show that she'd never got along with him. For one thing, she liked to go out to all the bright spots. He was about twice her age, a broker, and liked to stay at home. They had quarreled on the very night that he was shot. Not only that, he had taken $90,000 of insurance out in her name.

The jury took twenty minutes to decide what to do with her.

'Not guilty,' they said.

The picture showed her smiling after the verdict, standing with her lawyer, a big bouquet in her arms.

The flowers were roses.

The lawyer was Mark Bannister.

As a lawyer he was a lot different than as just a man. He came in to see me, looking very pleased with himself, smooth and suave in striped gray trousers and black coat, a white carnation in his coat lapel.

'Sorry I couldn't see you before,' he said briskly. 'Naturally I want to do all I can for you.'

I said: 'I was hoping you'd come and see me.'

'Of course you know the Grand Jury has already indicted you for the shooting of Lee Grisby. They had no alternative, since you had signed the confession. But now supposing you tell me all about it.'

'There isn't much to tell.'

'If you'd only seen me before you signed the confession—'

'I just told them what happened,' I said. 'Then they asked me to sign it.'

He shook his head.

'It isn't what happened,' he said. 'Obviously.'

'No?'

'No! If I'm going to help you – and you must see what an odd position that puts me in, defending a man on trial for killing my own law partner – you're going to have to tell me everything.'

'But—'

'The State will try to prove that you killed Grisby with intent, that the whole thing was premeditated, even to your preparations for leaving the country, and that there was no accident to it. The motive they'll try to establish, of course, will be robbery. They'll try to prove that by your possession of the five thousand dollars – money known to have been withdrawn by Grisby *while you looked on.*'

I decided to test him out.

'Do you think I killed him for the money?' I asked.

'That's just it – I don't think so. And I can't, if I'm to defend you. Because unless I can convince myself that you killed him *accidentally*, as you said in the confession, I'd have to withdraw even before I begin. A good many of my colleagues would be justified, otherwise, in feeling that I ought better to be on the prosecution side of this case.

You may not know it, but there's a fine matter of ethics involved here.'

'Well,' I said, 'it *was* an accident.'

'You shot him just the way you said?'

'Yes. We were parked on the little hill above the beach, just trying to cool off. Then we thought we heard a sound and Grisby said maybe it was someone to hold us up. He was afraid because of the five thousand dollars he was carrying.'

'What was he going to do with the money, did he happen to mention it?'

'No, he didn't say.'

'Why did you go into the bank with him when he drew the money out?'

'He asked me to.'

'But why?'

'I don't know. He just asked me to and I did.'

He shook his head again to show that he didn't believe it. But he didn't stop to argue.

'All right,' he said, 'go on with the story.'

'Well, when we heard the sound, Grisby said to get the gun out of the side-pocket of the car, just in case. I reached in and got it, but I'd hardly taken it out when it went off.'

'In the confession you said that you were getting out of the car and that you slipped or something, causing the gun to go off.'

I tried to remember what I had said about that, and couldn't.

'It all happened at once,' I said. 'I took the gun out, opened the door and started to get out all at the same time. I don't know how it happened to go off, but when I saw he was dead I got scared and dragged him out of the car into the bushes near there. Then a lot of people came up to see what the shooting was all about.'

'They said you were coming up from the pier when they came on the scene.'

'Yes, that's right. I'd gone down there to wash my hands.'

He made a clucking sound.

'There wouldn't have been time. The first man got there only seconds after the shot had been fired. His statement is backed up by statements of others who followed him. The State would trip you up on almost everything you've said so far. But go ahead, I want to hear your own version of this.'

'Well, that's about all. After the people had left, I went back to Grisby and took the money. I knew it wouldn't do him any good any more—'

'And then you threw his body into the Sound?'

I did some fast thinking.

'I don't know how I happened to say that in the confession, except that they were all pushing me pretty hard. I guess I was just rattled. What really happened was that I left him right there, in the bushes. I was sure he was dead. It wouldn't have done any good to get him to a doctor. And if I brought him back, and said it was an accident, I didn't know if anyone would believe me.'

'So you left him there. Then what did you do?'

'I drove the car back to the garage.'

'Right away?'

'As fast as I could.'

'And stayed there?'

'Yes – until the police came.'

'Why did you run away when they came?'

'I was afraid they'd come to arrest me for killing him. Even if it *was* an accident, they might make it tough for me. So I cleared out.'

'But didn't you stop to think how that would damage your case?'

'I was pretty rattled, all right. But I gave myself up – don't forget that!'

'Yes, that's something.'

'And I made the confession by myself, too – they didn't have to drag it out of me.'

He ran a thin, sharp finger down his nose.

'Yes! Speaking of that – McCracken says you made it almost eagerly. That's one of the reasons it's open to suspicion. Another reason is that you said you had thrown the body into the Sound, whereas it was found, dry, down on Wall Street!'

'I think I can explain that,' I said.

I told him McCracken's idea. That Grisby hadn't been dead, as I'd thought. That he'd come to, seen the speedboat tied up at the pier, and gone down to Wall Street himself. That by the time he'd got there he was so weak from loss of blood, probably, that he'd died almost as soon as he'd got onto the street, and before he could reach the office.

'From the shot accidentally discharged by you on the beach?'

'Yes.'

'With the gun that was in the side-pocket of the car?'

'Yes.'

'After taking himself down in the speedboat that was later found *back at the pier?*'

'Yes.'

He put on his hat and started to leave. Then he stopped and turned to look at me, leaning hard on his cane.

'Do you *want* to go to the chair?' he asked. 'Is that it?'

'What do you mean – about the bullet?'

'About everything! I can't help you if you won't help yourself. I've been talking to McCracken. He says that the fatal bullet – the one that caused Grisby's death – couldn't possibly have come from the gun you said it did.'

'Yeah, I know . . .'

He came back and sat down again.

'Now tell me all about it,' he said. 'Everything.'

'Supposing I had had another gun,' I said, 'and had thrown it away after the shooting, would that go pretty hard against me?'

'I'd never get a jury to believe you hadn't shot him, if that's what you mean. Did you have another gun?'

'No, I didn't.'

'Then you didn't shoot him!'

'No.'

He drew back and stared at me.

'Then for God's sake, why did you say you did?'

I didn't say anything for a minute. I didn't know what to say, unless I accused him of having done it himself.

'Well, I'll tell you why,' he said. 'I'll tell you. You confessed to killing Grisby, a crime for which you thought they'd have less chance of convicting you, in a desperate attempt to get out of another crime – the murder of Broome!'

'No,' I said. 'I didn't kill Broome. That wasn't it at all.'

'How else can you explain it? Not that it was a very smart move on your part – it was a very foolish move. It just serves further to establish your guilt on both counts.'

'But you just said if I didn't have another gun, I couldn't have killed Grisby!'

'Yes, but I didn't say you didn't have another gun. You might have had. The thing is, what line of defense are we going to take? So far you haven't said a thing that would help me in the least. Now, why? What are you trying to conceal, unless you did kill him – and not accidentally?'

I decided I'd have to do something, and in a hurry. Otherwise he'd walk out on me sure.

'Can they really send me to the chair?' I asked. 'I mean, if they can't prove I didn't have another gun?'

'They certainly can. They can say you threw the other gun away in the swamp, or in the Sound. Did you?'

'No,' I said. 'There wasn't any other gun.'

'All right. That brings us right back where we were. You didn't shoot him. You couldn't have. Then why did you say you had?'

'Because I didn't know he was going to get killed,' I said.

He thought I was trying to be smart. His jaw snapped.

'You're playing with dynamite here,' he said. 'I'm telling you, they can convict you. The State has an air-tight case. Maybe you are innocent – if I didn't think you were, or at the worst that it was an accident and you were just being very dumb, I wouldn't be helping you now. But now you say you didn't shoot him at all – then why did you confess to it? Don't you realize how serious this is?'

'I told you, I didn't know he was going to get killed. It was supposed to be a fake murder.'

'A fake murder!'

'Yes. Grisby wanted to get away from his wife – she wouldn't give him a divorce. So he hired me to pretend to kill him accidentally – he gave me five thousand dollars to prove I'd killed him. He said the police couldn't do anything unless they could find the body, and that he'd be on his way to the South Seas, so I'd be absolutely safe. It all sounded pretty easy.'

He looked at me as though he couldn't believe he had heard right.

'Are you serious?' he asked.

'That's why I confessed,' I said. 'It was all part of the scheme. I never dreamed—'

'But Grisby wasn't married!'

My mouth fell open.

'He *wasn't!*'

'Of course not!'

'But—'

'The whole thing is ridiculous! If you think I'm going to go into court with a story like that, you're crazy.'

IV

Grisby not married!

I didn't know what to say.

'But that's the reason he gave me,' I said. 'Really.'

'All right. It may be true. It sounds just fantastic enough – just like some scheme that Grisby might think up. And it checks with certain facts I happen to know. Grisby was preparing to leave the country, I'm sure of that. He'd been putting his house in order for some time. But we can't use it. No jury in the world would believe it.'

'No, I guess not. Not if he didn't even have a *wife*. But that's what he said and that's why he gave me the five thousand, to help him get away from her. He said that was the only way. That's why he brought me into the bank with him, too – so I'd be sure of getting the money as soon as I went through with my part.'

Bannister was thinking.

'So then he *did* take the boat down to Wall Street himself. It fits, all right,' he said. 'It could be.'

'Oh, he took the boat down himself, all right. I saw him leave. I was supposed to wait until he was out a way, and then fire the shot into the sand. The idea was to make people think afterwards, when the police learned he'd disappeared, that I really *had* shot him and thrown his body into the Sound. That was the story I was to confess to.'

'Then why did you run away? Before you said it was because you were afraid they might not think it was an accident. That doesn't hold with the new story you're telling me.'

'I got scared when I heard the police coming. I thought maybe there was some trick to it and that Grisby would cross me up, so I tried to hide out in the swamp. Then I got to thinking, and I figured the best thing to do was give myself up and go through with it just as we'd planned. So I came back and made the confession.'

'Well, at least that's a story I can believe,' he said. 'But the jury would never believe it, and we can't use it.'

I saw that easily enough – now that I knew Grisby hadn't even been married.

'Well, then what can we use?' I asked.

'The accident plea is all we have. It isn't good, but we can say you did have another gun, and that you threw it away, and we can say that Grisby then took the boat down to Wall Street of his own accord and died there from your shot.'

'I should say I shot him when I didn't?'

'It's your only chance.'

'Why can't we take back the confession and try to show that *somebody else* killed him?'

'Oh, we'll plead you 'Not Guilty,' don't worry about that. It's a law in this state that a man on trial for his life can't plead guilty, anyway. But I'm in favor of letting the confession stand. I wasn't before. They might laugh the accident plea right out of court. But what else have we?'

'Maybe we can find the one who really did kill him. That would solve everything.'

'That's easy to say; hard to do. Where would we start? The trial would be over before we could begin.'

'Maybe not.'

'What do you mean? Have you any ideas?'

'One.'

'Who?'

'You!'

Bannister ran his finger up and down his nose again. He didn't seem surprised, just puzzled.

'Why do you think I might have killed him?' he asked quietly. 'Why, Laurence?'

'Maybe to keep him from killing you.'

'Why would he want to kill me?'

'I don't know.'

'It's ridiculous, then, isn't it, to suppose I might have killed him?'

'I guess I just can't think of anyone else who might have done it.'

'Don't you suppose the police have looked into the possibility that I might have done it? It's the first thing they did when they found you couldn't have been down on Wall Street yourself. And they've given me a complete bill of health.'

'Did they look into the Broome angle, too?'

'Of course they did. They know I couldn't have killed Broome – I was out in the swamp all the time, helping them look for you. Besides, the two crimes are definitely related. No, Laurence; I'm glad you brought this up, just to clear it from your own mind; we'll have to work together, you know.'

'Do you think they'll try me for Broome's killing?'

'You don't need to worry about Broome – not yet. They're sure to try you on the Grisby matter first. And as for that – well, we'll just have to take our chances on the accident plea!'

He left me with a lot of thinking to do.

Grisby not married! That was a jolt. And Bannister – I wasn't even sure about him any more.

Supposing he hadn't killed Grisby, or Broome. Supposing he hadn't seen my letter and didn't know a thing about Grisby's plan to murder him. I would be in a fine fix if I told him about it, and about how I'd let Grisby talk me into helping him carry the plan through. Then he'd refuse to do a thing for me – and I wanted him to, now. Things were closing in on me. I was beginning to get scared. And he'd got the society woman off, hadn't he? That was an 'accident,' too, just like mine.

So I kept still. I knew I could always spring the truth, if the accident plea didn't work.

I waited, not *really* scared yet, but plenty worried. I waited, and watched to see what would happen.

V

Elsa came to see me often. She came whenever she thought the coast was clear.

Nobody knew who she was. She always wore the little hat with the veil, and the name she used on the visitors' list was Sheila Stewart.

The guards couldn't figure it out. Even with the veil they could tell how beautiful she was. She always dressed beautifully, too. And who was I, anyway? A chauffeur! A young punk who'd confessed to one killing and probably had done two.

The Whim Slayer!

The papers had got hold of that now and were playing it up strong. They'd found out about Sheila Stewart, too; they called her the 'Mystery Woman.' They didn't know yet, of course, that she was really Elsa Bannister – but they might find out.

And still she came to see me.

'I have to, Laurence,' she said. 'I have to, don't you see? I feel, somehow . . . well, as though I were responsible for your being here. If I hadn't kept you from leaving that night—'

Tears blurred her eyes. Her lips trembled.

'That was the best thing that ever happened to me,' I said. 'Bannister was right – I'd been asleep before. You woke me up. Now I'm living. Now I'm *alive!*'

We looked at each other, and the screen began to vibrate again.

'Your trial comes up in another week,' she said. 'Marco says the State plans to rush it right through. They're so sure . . . so sure . . .'

And there she was, crying again.

'He doesn't think I have much of a chance, does he?'

'He says he's certain you didn't do it.'

'Just the same, he wants me to stand by the confession. To keep to my story that I killed Grisby, but accidentally. He says the jury might believe that – and that they'd never believe I hadn't shot him at all, with all the evidence against me.'

'He says you told a wild story—'

'About Grisby paying me five thousand dollars to make believe I'd killed him? Well, he did.'

'But he said you did it to help Grisby get away from his wife!'

'That's what Grisby told me. How was I to know he didn't have a wife?'

'But don't you see? Marco was right – the jury would never believe such a story!'

I'd thought about that myself.

'Well, we could leave the wife part of it out,' I said. 'We could say he wanted the police to believe he was dead for another reason.'

'I suppose you might . . . but it would have to be a good reason. Otherwise the jury would think you were saying anything that came into your head, just to save yourself.'

That was when I began to think that maybe they *wouldn't* believe it, maybe they wouldn't believe anything I said. If I told them I had lied in the first place, about having killed Grisby, wouldn't they think I was lying even more if I changed the story to say I hadn't? I'd have so much more reason for lying, with the chair before me . . .

'I'll tell you the truth,' I said. 'Grisby did give me the five thousand dollars to pretend I'd killed him. He did say he wanted to get away from his wife, and that it was worth giving up everything, just to do that. But there was another reason, too – and a good one.'

I had to tell somebody. She was the only real friend I had, the only one I *could* tell.

'What – what was that?' she asked.

'Grisby wanted to make it look like he was dead,' I told her, 'because he wanted to kill somebody else. And he knew they'd never suspect him if I could "prove" that I'd killed him – accidentally, of course.'

Her eyes, behind the veil, became very large.

'Lee *Grisby?*' she said.

'Sure – Grisby.'

'I'd never believe it! Why—'

'Oh, it's true, all right! He wanted to kill someone.'

'But – why, it's ridiculous!'

'Just the same—'

'Who – who was he going to kill? Did he tell you that?'

'Yes. He said he was going to kill Bannister.'

'Marco?'

She couldn't believe it.

'But that's impossible!' she said. 'Don't you see how impossible it is? They'd been partners for years. They'd never even had a single quarrel. Oh, I'm sure you're mistaken. Not Marco!'

I began to think that maybe all Grisby's talk about killing Bannister had been a trick too – just like the wife business – a blind to cover up something else. But what?

'Well, that's what he said.'

'But what could he possibly gain from it?'

'He said he was going to get a lot of money out of it – enough to keep him in velvet for years.'

'But how would he get the money? Don't you see, there *must* be some mistake? Even if he told you that—'

'Well, I guess if you don't believe it, I'd never get a jury to!'

'And where was he going to go? Where could he hide?'

'He was going down to the South Seas.'

'The South Seas? Why, the whole thing's fantastic. Laurence! . . . You haven't told this to anyone else, have you? Not to the police?'

'Not yet.'

'And not to Marco – Mr Bannister?'

'Oh, Lord, no!'

'Well, you mustn't – or the police, either! It's the worst possible thing you could say.'

'But it may be my only chance!'

'Oh, I know, I know . . . but don't you see? Even if it's true – particularly if it's true – if you said you had agreed to help him kill somebody else, do you suppose they would hesitate to think you had killed *him?* They'd be sure of it, then.'

That's when I began to get really scared.

'But I can't believe it,' she said, 'I can't believe either that Lee Grisby would do such a thing, or that you would help him!'

If it hadn't been for her I wouldn't have. I had to make her see my side of it.

'Well, I wasn't really going to kill anyone,' I said. 'I was just going to make it look that way. All I was supposed to do was fire a shot into the sand. That's all I did. And now they're trying to send me to the chair for it! For a shot in the sand!'

She was silent for a while, trying to understand all this, and not having an easy time of it, I could tell.

'So that's why you think Marco killed him,' she said. 'You think he did it in self-defense?'

'I can't see how else it could have happened.'

'But if it was self-defense, wouldn't he say so? Why would he try to hide it? He wouldn't need to! No jury in the world would convict him. But you—'

'Five minutes,' said the guard. 'Time's up.'

She brought me fruit, and saw that I had good meals. She brought me newspapers and books.

So everything was all right. I'd been afraid that maybe she'd hold it against me, being in a scheme with Grisby to kill her husband. Because she believed it, finally, even though she couldn't understand it. But she believed it only after she'd found out something – something I hadn't known myself. There had been a hundred-thousand-dollar partnership insurance policy between Grisby and Bannister.

'But what I can't understand,' she said, 'is how he expected to collect on it, if he was supposed to be dead himself?'

'And now Bannister gets that money?'

'Oh, yes.'

That seemed the height of something, I didn't know what. The whole thing was getting more mixed up every minute.

'Supposing they both had died at the same time,' I said, 'what would have happened then? Who would have got the money?'

'Well, I suppose if Grisby had been married, part of it would have gone to his wife, too. But this way it would have gone to me. So he couldn't have profited in the least by killing Marco.'

'No, I guess not.'

'Laurence, why did you do this?' she asked suddenly.

I nearly jumped.

'Kill Grisby, you mean? But—'

'No, I know you didn't do that. I believe you. I mean, why did you agree to go in with him on this? Oh, I know, he offered you five thousand dollars, but don't you see how foolish you were? Could all this possibly be worth five thousand dollars?'

'No,' I said. 'But I wasn't going to do it, either. That night when you met me outside the garage, when I was going away, I said I was going because I wasn't cut out to be a chauffeur. I was a sailor. I said I was going back to sea. Well, I was going back, but not for that reason. I was afraid if I didn't go through with it, Grisby would get me, too. So I was clearing out – fast.'

'And I stopped you! Oh, Laurence, if you'd only told me.'

'I did start to tell Bannister. I wrote him a letter. But when we came back from the beach, I – well, I tore the letter up.'

'But why?'

'Because it wasn't *me* that was going to kill anyone. If Bannister couldn't look out for himself . . . And then, most of all, there was *you*.'

I could hear her catch her breath.

'I see . . .'

'That's why I did it, really. I thought everything would work out – differently.'

'Oh, Laurence—'

'You said yourself you thought Bannister would be better off dead. Then he wouldn't be worrying so much about his leg.'

'I – I shouldn't have said that. I was furious . . .'

'But you meant it, didn't you?'

'Please, Laurence—'

'You did mean it!'

'I guess I did – at the moment. Sometimes, when he broods, and is irritable—'

'You're not in love with him, I know that.'

'No. I guess I never was, really. I guess it was always just – pity. It still is. If it hadn't been for that I would have left him a dozen times.

It would have hurt him too terribly. Besides, he would never give me a divorce. He'd fight it if it took every penny he had.'

'But what are we going to do when I get out? If,' I said, 'he gets me out?'

'I don't know. We'll have to think about that – when the time comes.'

Bannister came in so soon after she had left that it made my hair curl. I wondered if he'd seen her.

'Well,' he said, 'it's all set. The trial comes up tomorrow. The State has a strong case, but we can beat it. That's what I want you to keep in your mind – no matter how black they make things look for you, cling to the accident plea.'

'Yes,' I said.

'The State will charge you with murder in the first degree. Our line of defense will be excusable homicide – accident. Remember, it's the State's job to prove you guilty, not ours to prove you innocent. If you say you didn't shoot him at all, and try to prove your innocence, you'll simply be helping the State to prove your guilt – the weight of evidence to bear out their theory that you *did* shoot him, even though that evidence is only circumstantial, is too strong.'

'But if I'm innocent, they can't *prove* me guilty, can they?'

'They certainly can. They'll evolve a theory of the shooting, then bring up facts to bear that theory out. When they get through with their witnesses, there won't be a single man on the jury who'll believe you didn't shoot Lee Grisby. We'd be foolish to dispute it; we have no proof that you didn't. Of course, they have no actual proof that you did, either. But the weight of evidence is on their side.'

'We can prove I didn't do it with the gun I had – McCracken said so. He said I *couldn't* have done it with that gun!'

'Yes, but we can't prove you didn't have another gun. How could we? And they'll say you did – and they'll seem to prove it by the very fact that we can't disprove it. Besides, as I said, they will have convinced the jury, through their witnesses, that you did shoot him. And since they wouldn't believe it if we said you didn't, they'd hesitate to believe us when we said it was an accident. No, the issue we'll have to stand or fall on is whether the shooting was *premeditated* or *accidental* – and I think I can throw enough doubt on that score to prevent your conviction. At any rate, it's our only hope.'

So I went on trial for my life claiming to have killed a man I hadn't killed – and hoping they'd believe me, but not to the extent where they'd send me to the chair for it.

PART FOUR

I

The courtroom was crowded and noisy. There were a lot of women, but I saw Elsa almost at once. She wasn't wearing the veil this time, not even a hat. Sunlight shooting down from a high window lighted her red hair. She smiled and I smiled back.

Bannister was sitting at a table up near the judge's bench. He looked around to see what I was smiling at. Elsa was folding a handkerchief in her lap. He turned back to me frowning and drew out a chair beside his own.

'Scared?' he asked.

'A little,' I said.

'Well, don't be. Sit down. Don't smile, but don't look pessimistic, either.'

The judge was rapping for order.

'That's Judge Ditchburne,' said Bannister. 'He'll see that you get a square deal.'

The judge had scraggly white hair and brows over a red face. A sour smile was on his lips.

A voice droned: 'Hear ye, hear ye, hear ye. All ye who have business draw near, give attention, and ye shall be heard.'

'The main thing today,' said Bannister, 'will be to choose the jury. That may or may not take time, depending upon how much sifting Galloway and I have to do.'

'Who's Galloway?'

'He's the District Attorney. Ordinarily he wouldn't be prosecuting the case himself, but he wants the publicity on this one. It's enough out of the ordinary to get a lot of attention. Besides, he's sure he's going to win it.'

'Which one is he?'

He nodded to a man in a brown suit over at another table, standing with his back to us, going through a lot of papers. He was a short, bull-necked man with big shoulders and a completely bald head that gave him a streamlined effect – trimmed for action. When he turned around I saw that he had a big jaw and large brown eyes with a twinkle. He smiled at me and looked up at the judge. This was the man who was going to do his best to send me to the chair.

The courtroom quieted down. The business of picking the jurors began.

Galloway didn't seem much interested in who the jurors were, as long as they had nothing against sending me to the chair. Bannister turned some of them down, but I couldn't tell why. Finally, just after the adjournment for lunch, they had twelve of them all sitting up in the jury box – two women and ten men, all freshly scrubbed and dressed to kill.

Then they brought me up to the bar to plead.

'Not guilty,' I said.

I went back and sat down beside Bannister.

Galloway didn't lose any time. He swung right into action, getting more and more worked up each moment.

'May it please the Court,' he began. 'We are here in the matter of the People of New York against Laurence Planter.'

It was funny to hear my name in that place, with those twelve people looking at me. And the more Galloway talked, the worse it was.

'The defense will try to delude you,' he said to the jurors, 'into the belief that this outrageous crime against society was committed by accident. I shall prove that nothing could be further from the truth. I shall prove that he was preparing to leave the country. I shall prove that he saw the unhappy victim of his avarice, Lee Grisby, draw five thousand dollars from the bank. And I shall prove that he killed him to obtain this sum – practically in the presence of witnesses. These witnesses will speak to you for themselves, testifying under oath. You need have no hesitation in accepting their word; you need have no hesitation in returning a verdict of guilty of murder in the first degree!'

If he had said nothing else, if the jurors had gone right out then and there and taken a vote on it, they would have said 'Guilty!' I knew it. I knew I was sunk. There wasn't anything we could say that would change it, unless I told the truth. And Bannister had said I couldn't do that; it would sink me quicker than anything else we could say. So what was left? I didn't know.

Galloway's voice rang out: 'Call Dr Colbert.'

Cold shivers went up and down my spine.

Dr Colbert, it turned out, was the medical examiner. He proved, to everyone's satisfaction, that Grisby was dead.

'And how was this death inflicted, Dr Colbert?'

'By a bullet entering the heart.'

'Fired straight or from the side?'

'From the side – the left side.'

'At what distance would you say?'

'At a very short distance. Powder burns visible on the coat suggested that the pistol was held very close.'

'The shot could, then, in your opinion, have been fired by one sitting beside Mr Grisby at the wheel of a car?'

Bannister came to his feet.

'Objection. Question can only elicit opinion, not fact,' he said.

Galloway looked at him in surprise.

'We are only trying to secure expert medical opinion,' he said, 'to bear out a statement given as fact by the defendant himself. In the confession I am about to read as soon as death and cause of death have been established—'

'Objection overruled,' the judge snapped. 'The District Attorney may proceed.'

'The witness may answer,' said Galloway.

'Very well. In my opinion the shot could most certainly have been fired by a person sitting on the left side of the deceased in a car.'

'That's all,' said Galloway. 'Your witness, Mr Bannister.'

'One question, for the records,' said Bannister.

Galloway was still frowning at him, puzzled.

'Counsel doesn't question there has been a death?' he asked.

'I should like to establish the exact means of death,' Bannister explained. 'Dr Colbert, can you tell me the caliber of the bullet removed from the deceased?'

'Yes. It was a .32.'

'Perhaps the District Attorney would be kind enough to offer it in evidence?'

Galloway picked the bullet up from the table. It had a tag on it.

Bannister took it, looked at the tag, and handed it up to Dr Colbert.

'Is this the bullet? The fatal bullet with which Lee Grisby was killed?'

'Yes.'

'Thank you, Dr Colbert. That is all.' He looked at the judge. 'If Your Honor please, I should like the Court to order the State to produce this bullet for introduction in evidence at the time of the presentation by the defense.'

Judge Ditchburne looked puzzled, too.

'Very well,' he said, after glancing at Galloway. 'It will be so marked.'

Bannister nodded to the medical examiner and sat down.

'What's the idea?' I asked. 'Are you going to try to prove I didn't shoot him, after all?'

'Oh, no. The trick is to establish a reasonable doubt in the minds of the jury that you might have done it purposely. I want to be able to show that the gun found in the car doesn't match with the bullet taken from Grisby. It won't prove that you didn't have another gun, but it will prove that the District Attorney's case isn't as air-tight as he'll try to make the jury believe. If it isn't air-tight, there's a reasonable doubt. That's all.'

Galloway next read the confession I had made. It had been reworded, with a lot of technical language, to make it hold up in court, but it still said that I had shot Grisby accidentally and then dumped him into the Sound. We had tried to change this to read that I had left him on the beach, but the best they'd do was to put it into a second confession.

The jurors were so interested they sat with their mouths open, listening to every word.

After he'd read the first confession, Galloway called a policeman to the stand. His name was Peters. He was from the Old Slip Station down near Wall Street, and he had found the body.

'You were on duty at the foot of Wall Street on the night of August twelfth?'

'Yes, sir.'

'Tell the jury, please, exactly what you saw and heard.'

'It was twenty minutes after eleven. The street was deserted. I was down at the South Street end looking around the Skyport when I saw a body stretched out on the pavement. I ran over and saw that it was Mr Grisby, of the law firm of Bannister and Grisby.'

A buzz went up. Everyone turned to look at Bannister, to see if he was the same one. The jurors were all whispering back and forth.

'Continue, please,' said Galloway. 'What did you do then?'

'Without touching the body, except to see that he was dead – there was a pool of blood under him that was still wet – I turned in the report and told the night man in Mr Grisby's office building, right up the street, what had happened. He identified him, too, and then went back to get Mr Bannister, who was waiting for him up in their office. Mr Bannister came right down and we all stood and waited for the Homicide men to get there.'

'All right. Now a few questions, please. You say that you discovered the body at 11:20 P. M. How long before that had you been in the vicinity?'

'I turned into the street at eleven-ten.'

'You saw nothing out of the way? You heard nothing?'

'No, sir.'

'Did any cars pass you on the street?'

'On Wall Street? No, sir.'

'And you heard no shot?'

'No, sir. The street was very quiet.'

Galloway turned to the jury, then back to the witness.

'Let me make sure I understand that. *You say that you heard no shot.* Yet, from the condition of the blood, which you have testified was still wet when you came upon the body, Lee Grisby had been dead only a short time. So we know that death must have come on Wall Street, but not, it would appear, from a shot fired on Wall Street, or you would have heard it. Isn't that right?'

'Objection!' said Bannister. 'The shot might have been fired before the officer came within hearing distance and Mr Grisby still be dead only a short time, or the murderer might have used a silencer.'

'Mr Bannister is correct,' said the judge. 'No definite conclusion can be drawn from the fact that the officer heard no shot. Strike the District Attorney's remarks from the record.'

Galloway stretched out his arms, palms out in a pleading gesture.

'But, Your Honor – the fact that no shot was heard simply bears out the statement made by the defendant himself, in his confession, that Mr Grisby was actually shot some distance away – in fact, on the beach. But we will return to that later. Right now we will continue with the officer's testimony, as he is anxious to get home to his wife and family before he returns to duty.'

Peters looked at him and started to say something, but Galloway rushed right on. His idea was to get the jury sore at Bannister if he took up a lot of time in cross-examination, and he didn't want Peters spoiling it.

'Now we come to a very important point, Mr Peters. Please tell the jury the condition of Mr Grisby's clothes at the moment you came upon the body.'

'Why, they seemed to be in good condition, except for the blood, of course.'

'Were they wet or dry?'

'Oh, I see what you mean. They were dry.'

'Dry!' Galloway whirled around. 'Dry! Yet the defendant said in his confession that he had thrown the body into the Sound!'

'I object!' said Bannister.

'Grounds?'

'On the grounds that a subsequent confession made by my client withdraws the statement that the body was thrown into the Sound. The District Attorney, it seems to me, is taking unfair advantage of a situation which he knows has been rectified.'

'Objection sustained,' the judge said. 'The District Attorney's last remark will also be stricken from the record.'

Galloway shrugged. He looked at the jury to make sure they'd got it, anyway. They had.

'Very well,' he said. 'The fact remains that the clothes were dry.

Now, Mr Peters, was there anything else that struck you at the time of the discovery of the body?'

'Yes, sir, there was something. Mr Grisby was lying face down, with his arms thrown out. His hat had rolled to one side. But in his right hand was a cap – held so tight that the Homicide men had a hard time getting it loose when they came.'

'What kind of cap?'

Peters wet his lips and looked at me.

'A chauffeur's cap,' he said.

Galloway went to the table and snatched up the cap Grisby had taken from me when he'd dashed for the boat.

'Is this it?' he asked.

'It looks like it.'

Galloway turned, waving the cap.

'Think of it!' he said. 'Here is a man mortally wounded – struck down in the prime of life, yet with the quickness and brilliance of thought that characterized his whole career at the bar, snatching the evidence that would send his murderer to the chair! So that a competent jury, sitting in trial upon that murderer, might avenge his death without the slightest fear of error or of possible miscarriage of justice. Watch!'

He came over and slapped the cap on my head, tight.

'Objection!' shouted Bannister. He got to his feet so quickly he wrenched his game leg. Pain shot through his face. He grabbed the table and held on.

'Of course defense counsel objects,' said Galloway. 'The cap fits!'

'I object to the tactics employed by the District Attorney,' Bannister snapped. 'He is supposed to be conducting a direct examination; his opportunity to sum up will come later. Besides, such dramatics are entirely unnecessary. The defense has never denied that the cap in question belonged to the defendant. But to say that it is the defendant's because it fits is ridiculous. The cap is of standard size. It could fit ten million others as easily. I ask that the District Attorney's conclusions be stricken from the record as being ill-timed, unfounded, and immaterial.'

'Objection overruled,' said Judge Ditchburne. 'The evidence, I should say, is material. But I must caution the District Attorney to confine himself, until such time as he is ready for his summation, to direct examination.'

Galloway shrugged.

'I offer this cap in evidence as Exhibit A,' he said, yanking it off. 'It is not only highly material, but as I shall attempt to show, it is *positive proof* that we have here no mere case of accidental shooting, as the defense would like us to believe, and as attested to in the defendant's confession, but an out-and-out case of first degree *murder*.'

'That's not true,' I yelled. 'I—'

Bannister put a hand on my arm and kept me down.

'Let him finish,' he said. 'Our turn will come later.'

'Will you put me on the stand?'

'No, I can't do that – it would give him just the chance he wants to cross-examine you. But don't worry; it won't be necessary.'

Galloway turned to Peters, who was twisting his own cap around.

'That's all,' he said. 'Your witness, Mr Bannister.'

Bannister stood up slowly, thinking.

'No questions – except, yes. One.' He looked at Peters, who was half way out of the chair. 'Of course I don't want to keep you from your wife and children, any more than the District Attorney, who was so concerned about them a moment ago. But I would like to ask one question. *Have* you a wife and children, Mr Peters?'

'Well—'

Peters looked at Galloway. Then he started to smile.

'No,' he said.

A laugh went up all over the courtroom. Judge Ditchburne banged his gavel. Galloway got red, but tried to shrug it off.

'Thank you,' said Bannister to Peters. 'You may step down.'

He looked at Galloway and came back and sat beside me, smiling. You could still hear people laughing.

'All right!' said Galloway. 'This is a very serious occasion for the State, even if it doesn't seem important or worthy of serious conduct by the defense. Perhaps Mr Bannister realizes the futility of his case. Or perhaps he is bored with the proceedings. Well, we will make things more interesting from now on. Our next witness is a man of unimpeachable integrity, honest, fearless and public-spirited in the extreme. Although he may be somewhat surprised at the request, I am sure he will not hesitate to testify. Call Mark Bannister!'

'Mark Bannister!' droned the crier.

A murmur started in the courtroom, swelled to a thunder clap as the judge's gavel hit the bench. I turned around to look at Elsa. She tried to smile, to encourage me, but she was plenty worried, I could tell. Well, I was worried, too. It looked like I didn't have a chance. And now Galloway was even trying to put Bannister, my own lawyer, on the witness stand!

Bannister stood up, roaring mad.

'All right!' he snapped back at Galloway. 'I'll take the stand!'

'One moment,' said Judge Ditchburne. 'I think that the defendant has something to say about that.' He looked at me. 'I must tell you that it is within your discretion to refuse to allow defense counsel to place your case in jeopardy by exposing himself to the prosecution's questioning – or, if he does do so, with or without your consent, to secure, or have the Court appoint, new counsel. If you care to discuss the matter before making a decision, the Court will order a brief recess. What does the defendant say?'

Almost I missed a chance here to do something good. It was all Greek to me, the whole business, and for a minute I didn't know what to say. But then I saw this chance, and before I knew it I said, all in one breath:

'No, I don't want any other lawyer if that's what you mean, and I'm not afraid of having Mr Galloway ask him questions, because there's nothing to be afraid of. I haven't done anything.'

I was out of breath and I knew my ears were red but I felt pretty proud of myself, all right, like you always do when you've said the right thing at the right time. But I was worried, don't think I wasn't.

II

Some newspaper men behind me were whispering about what was going on.

'Hey, Joe! What is this? Galloway can't make Bannister testify against his own *client*, can he?'

'It's a new one on me. This whole trial gets screwier and screwier every minute.'

'Why, if I was Bannister, I'd have busted him one.'

'I guess he doesn't have to testify – Galloway just asked him to and he agreed.'

'Well, I'm damned if I would have. Why, he's going to be under oath! And I always thought he was smart!'

'He is smart. Either he's got something up his sleeve or he knows Galloway could make him testify, anyway, even if he refused now. And that would look bad. Don't forget, the kid was his chauffeur. He's not being put on the stand as his lawyer, but as his boss. I'm not sure about this – it's just a guess. But it's a good one, all right – a lawyer testifying in his own case, against his own client!'

'Yeah, it's a good one, all right.'

Good, hell, where did they think I was going to come out in all this?

Bannister clumped up to the stand. The jurors screwed up their foreheads at the funny way he walked. You could see they held it against him, somehow.

'Do you swear to tell the truth, the whole truth, and nothing but the truth?'

'I do.'

Bannister got up into the chair and sat glowering down at Galloway. His face was dark, angered, his jaw set. He tried to cover up his twisted leg so it wouldn't look so awkward. He couldn't. It seemed to hang loose, disconnected.

Now there wasn't a sound in the whole courtroom.

Galloway got Bannister's name, address and profession, all as though he'd never seen him before.

'Now, Mr Bannister,' he said, 'on the night of August twelfth, you were in your office down on Wall Street?'

'Yes.'

'You were waiting for Mr Grisby, who had gone out to your home to get some papers. As I understand it, these papers had an important bearing on the case on which you were working? Is that true?'

'Yes. He had left them out there by mistake, and suggested he go out and get them.'

'At what time did you realize that Mr Grisby wasn't coming back?'

'At 11:35, when Mr Marek, the night watchman, came to tell me that Mr Grisby was lying dead out in the street. I immediately accompanied him downstairs to where Mr Grisby was lying. I identified him.'

'You noticed the cap in Mr Grisby's hand?'

'Yes.'

'What was your first comment on seeing the cap?'

'I was surprised. I said, "It looks like my chauffeur's. He must have driven him down here."'

'Didn't you say also that he must have killed him?'

'I said it looked as though he must have, since his cap was there and yet he himself was no longer in the vicinity.'

'Didn't you suggest that a search for him be made at once?'

'Naturally. If my chauffeur were guilty, I wanted him apprehended. After all, Mr Grisby was my partner.'

'Of course. You wanted to avenge his death – it was your duty, just as it is my duty. Now, not only that, but I imagine you felt a certain sense of responsibility, having hired and trusted the defendant, Laurence Planter, who later showed his gratitude by killing your own partner.'

Bannister just looked at him.

'I wonder,' said Galloway, 'just what you know about him to justify that trust? Surely he gave you some character references at the time you hired him?'

'No. It never occurred to me to ask for them.'

'How did you happen to hire him?'

'I needed a new chauffeur. I had discharged the old one for drunkenness the day before Laurence Planter turned up on my beach. Laurence was looking for work. He was young and strong. He had his whole life before him.'

'But didn't you even ask him about himself?'

'I questioned him a little of course. I found that he had been a sailor and had seen much of life, but – call it innocence if you want – that he had somehow managed to keep the taint of life outside himself.'

'So you hired him on faith?'

'Yes – on faith.'

'Well, now, Mr Bannister,' Galloway went on, 'you say that the defendant had no job when you hired him. He was simply drifting up and down along the Sound. In other words, he was a vagrant, wasn't he? A charge upon society?'

'He didn't have any money, if that's what you mean, no. At least, I assumed that he hadn't.'

'And how much did you pay him per week?'

'Eighteen dollars, plus room and board.'

'I see. At that rate, it would take him a good many years to save up five thousand dollars, wouldn't it?'

'I suppose it would.'

'And how long was Laurence Planter in your employ before the shooting of Lee Grisby?'

'About two months; I don't recall exactly.'

'He wasn't very content in his job, was he?'

Bannister looked pained, but he answered.

'I thought he was very content.'

'And then suddenly he wasn't content! Suddenly he was preparing to leave the country – to go back to sea. I wonder if you could enlighten us on that, Mr Bannister? Why did he want to leave?'

'I didn't know he wanted to leave.' Bannister turned to Judge Ditchburne. 'As defense counsel, I wish to object to the District Attorney's line of questioning. By indirection he is attempting to establish premeditation which does not exist.'

'Objection sustained,' said the judge.

'Very well. To return to the night of the crime, what did you say when you came out to your home with the police and found that Laurence Planter had run away?'

'I said, "That proves it. He did kill him."'

'And what did you say when the five thousand dollars was found hidden in his mattress?'

'I said, "That's the explanation. He killed him for the money."'

'You weren't surprised, were you?'

'In my profession, one ceases to be surprised at anything.'

'I can understand that. It's for the same reason, too, isn't it, that one ceases to put much trust in his fellowmen?'

'Possibly.'

'Yet you say you trusted Laurence Planter – and without knowing anymore about him than that he had been a sailor?'

'All I can say is that I did trust him. Obviously.'

Galloway lashed a sharp finger at him.

'Then why did you hire the detective Broome?'

Bannister jerked up. His face whitened.

'We live in a rather deserted section,' he began.

'One minute, please! You have lived there how long?'

'For eight years.'

'Eight years! For eight years you have lived in a "rather deserted" section of Long Island. And then, suddenly, only a few weeks after hiring the defendant, you feel called on to keep a detective on the premises!'

'Your Honor! I fail to see what possible connection the District Attorney's present line of questioning can have in this case. If I had not trusted my chauffeur, I would have dismissed him. Certainly I would not have gone to the expense of hiring a detective to watch him.'

Judge Ditchburne nodded.

'Can the District Attorney justify his present questioning?'

'Your Honor, I believe that the hiring of the detective Broome has a direct bearing on this case, and propose to show what that bearing is – now.'

'Very well.'

'I propose to show also that the defendant was hired because of his good looks and general physique and because he could *not* be trusted.'

'Proceed.'

'Isn't it true, Mr Bannister, that you had used the detective Broome in certain of your cases having to do with divorce cases?'

'I am not in the habit of accepting such cases.'

'No, but you have handled a number, haven't you?'

'Yes.'

'And you found it expedient to hire Broome to help procure evidence, in spite of the fact that his fees were high.'

'Yes.'

'You found it expedient because you knew his whole reputation and training had been in the procuring of such evidence?'

'Yes.'

'And you mean to tell us that you would hire a man trained in divorce actions, receiving high fees, *merely to watch your house?*'

'Partly, yes.'

'What do you mean, "partly"?'

Bannister looked at the judge.

'I refuse to answer on the grounds—'

Galloway plunged in.

'Exactly what I thought! You didn't hire him to watch your house at all. *You hired him to watch your wife.* You didn't trust her with the new chauffeur – but you wouldn't fire him, either. You *wanted* to leave them together – you wanted *evidence.* That's why you hired Broome to watch – instead of firing Laurence. Isn't that true – isn't it?'

'No!' said Bannister. 'I never had any thought of having Laurence watched.'

'Whom *did* you want watched?'

Bannister didn't answer. He just scowled angrily.

Judge Ditchburne broke in.

'I fail to see any connection between that and the case at hand, as the District Attorney promised to show.'

'The connection would be apparent if the questions were answered truthfully.'

'I think, then, since Mr Bannister has declined to answer on perfectly legal grounds, that the present line of questioning had best be dropped.'

'That's all then,' said Galloway. 'Your witness, Mr Bannister.'

Bannister climbed down off the witness chair and stood in front of the jury.

'As defense counsel,' he said, 'I should like to ask the witness, myself, that is, a few questions. Why did I say, on seeing the cap in Lee Grisby's hand, that my chauffeur must have killed him? Because that seemed, at the moment, to be the logical explanation. Why did I suggest that a search be made for him at once? Was it because I feared he would leave the country, as the District Attorney would have you believe? No, it was because I sincerely desired his apprehension at the earliest possible moment, to clear up the mystery. When I went out to my home to look for him, with the police, and we found that he had run away, why did I say, "That proves it. He did kill Grisby"? Because it seemed perfectly obvious that he had committed the crime, otherwise why would he run away?

'Well, what is so damaging about that? He *did* shoot Grisby. He *did* run away. The defense has never claimed otherwise. The defendant has made two such confessions in which he freely admits it. But in each he contends that the shooting was an accident. Was it? I had to know. If I was to undertake his defense, I had to be certain in my own mind that it had been an accident – it was my own partner who was killed. After his voluntary surrender, I questioned him. I talked to him and was convinced that he had had no premeditated ideas of murder – that it *had* been an accident.

'I asked him, then, why he had told the police that he had thrown the body in the Sound, when obviously he hadn't, as it had been found dry on Wall Street. He explained that he had been rattled by the questions put to him by the police. He explained also why he had run away when they came. He was afraid that perhaps the police wouldn't believe that it had been an accident. But then he had decided that the most honorable course was to put his trust in them and in you, the jury – and he thereupon surrendered, out of his own innate sense of honor. That's all.'

Galloway smiled as Bannister came back to his chair.

'A very pretty speech,' he said getting up.

I had thought it was, too. For a minute I had begun to think that maybe Bannister could swing an acquittal, after all.

But then Galloway pulled a surprise.

'Call Mrs Bannister,' he said.

III

I knew what was coming, all right. So did Elsa. She walked to the witness stand with her head up, not looking at anyone. You could hear the jury gasp when they saw her, she looked so beautiful.

Galloway stood by while she was sworn in and then tried to make a hit by helping her up into the chair.

The first thing she did was to look over at me and smile. I tried to smile back.

Bannister flushed. He looked from one to the other of us. He couldn't make out just what was going on, but whatever it was he didn't like it.

Galloway smiled up at Elsa.

'Now, Mrs Bannister,' he said, 'I'd like you to tell the jury exactly what happened on the night of August eleventh, between the hours of ten and twelve.'

What he was talking about was the night before Grisby was shot, when Elsa and I had lain in each other's arms on the beach.

'It all seems blurred, somehow,' she said. 'I don't seem to recall much about the night of – the night of August eleventh.'

'Then perhaps it will refresh your memory,' said Galloway, 'if I remind you that this was the night before Lee Grisby's murder.'

'Oh . . . yes.'

'It might refresh your memory still further to tell you that it was also the night on which Laurence Planter was making final arrangements to leave the country.'

'Objection,' said Bannister. 'Both to the word "murder" and to the inference that death of deceased was premeditated.'

'Sustained,' said Judge Ditchburne. 'The District Attorney knows better than to lead the witness.'

'I was only attempting to save time,' said Galloway. 'The facts will be brought out by the witness herself. To proceed, please, Mrs Bannister—'

'I remember now. On the night of August eleventh, at about eleven o'clock, I phoned for the car to be brought around to the house. It was hot; I couldn't sleep. I thought that a drive might help.'

'Was the call answered?'

She hesitated.

'No,' she said.

'So then what did you do?'

'I went to the garage to see what might have happened. The car was there. I thought then that perhaps Laurence was asleep and hadn't heard the phone.'

'And was he?'

'No. I started for the door. And just then he came out.'

'He came out. And what did he say?'

'I – I noticed that he had a bag with him. I asked him why he hadn't answered the phone.'

She was getting into deep water, all right, but she couldn't help herself. She was under oath.

'And he said – what?'

'He said that he was leaving.'

The way it came out, it was one of the most damaging things in the whole case.

'Were you surprised?' asked Galloway.

'Why, yes – I was.'

'Then he had never mentioned such a desire before?'

'No. He'd always seemed very pleased with his position. At least, I'd always thought that, without questioning it, really.'

'And what excuse did he give for wanting to leave?'

'He said that he wasn't cut out to be a chauffeur, he was a sailor. That was the first I had known of it.'

'I see. He was beginning to tire of the humdrum life of a chauffeur. He wanted life, action, adventure. He didn't want to struggle along all his life at a mere eighteen dollars a week. Is that it?'

'I – I don't know. I don't think it was the money, so much as—'

'But it was the money that led him to take the job, wasn't it?'

'I suppose so.'

'Then why did he decide to throw that money over?'

'I don't know. I told you, he wanted to go back to sea.'

'All right, then. Let's turn the question around. Why did he decide to stay, if he had his mind set on going back to sea? Everything shows that he was determined to go – his bag all packed, his stealthy exit, his very insolence in refusing to answer the phone. Why answer, if he was leaving? He wouldn't care about holding his job, then. And yet – and yet?'

'I'm sorry. I don't believe I understand the question.'

'And yet something caused him to stay. What was it?'

'Why – I suppose it was I who caused him to stay.'

I almost jumped, it was such a surprise.

'You! How?' asked Galloway.

'I told him that we were well pleased with his work as a chauffeur. I suggested that perhaps he was acting hastily, and that it would be wise to see my husband first – in the morning.'

'You hinted at an increase in pay?'

'No. I—'

'But that's what you wanted him to see Mr Bannister about, wasn't it?'

'No! I suggested that because I was sure that by then he'd have a different idea entirely. As a matter of fact, I didn't attach much importance to it at all, and I'm sure that's all it was – an impulse.'

'Just another whim, you mean?'

She didn't answer. She could have made it bad for me by saying that I'd been drinking. Not a word about that.

'Well, tell me, please, Mrs Bannister. You often saw him with Mr Grisby, didn't you?'

'Yes.'

'How did they seem to get along?'

'Very well. At least, Mr Grisby always spoke highly of Laurence. He expected big things of him.'

'But hardly what actually happened, I imagine. Now, on the night of August twelfth, what time did Mr Grisby arrive at the house?'

'About ten o'clock, the maid said. I wasn't there.'

'I see. At what time did you return?'

'It was about ten-thirty. Mr Grisby had already left, of course.'

'Did you call for the car from the station?'

'Yes. There was no answer.'

'So you walked from the station?'

'Yes. It isn't far to the house and I wanted the walk.'

'Was Laurence there when you got home?'

'No, not at that time.'

'How long does it take to drive to the station – and back?'

'Why, about five or ten minutes.'

'I see. And what time, Mrs Bannister, *did* Laurence return from driving Mr Grisby to the station?'

I looked right into her eyes, praying. But she didn't even hesitate.

'At about eleven – in fact, a little before. Not much. I saw his shadow moving in the garage. Something seemed wrong; I went over to ask him about it.'

'Did he seem nervous or frightened?'

'Yes – but he had been in an accident with the car. He had hit a truck. The whole front of the car was crushed in and the glass was broken. He was shaken up, naturally.'

'And did he say what had happened to Mr Grisby?'

'No.'

'Well, now, you say that he was about to leave on the night of August eleventh, and yet he was still there the next night, when Mr Grisby was killed. I suppose, then, that he did see Mr Bannister in the morning, as you suggested, and that he had been offered an increase in pay?'

'No; he didn't even talk to Mr Bannister about it. He was to drive us into town the next morning. As it happened, I came out to the car first. Laurence told me then that he had decided to stay. Naturally, that ended it; there was no reason to talk to Mr Bannister about it.'

'Did he tell you why he had changed his mind about leaving?'

'No, but as I said, it was only an impulse.'

'Then he didn't tell you his reason for staying?'

'No, but—'

'Well, now, let's get this straight. You say that on the night of August eleventh, you called for the car to go for a drive. Did you go?'

'Yes.'

'Did you stop anywhere along the way?'

'Why, yes. It was so hot, I decided to stop for a while at the beach.'

'I see. Did you leave the car and go onto the beach?'

'Yes . . . for a while.'

'And did Laurence go with you?'

Bannister was leaning forward tensely.

'Why, yes.'

Galloway almost hissed the next question.

'He kissed you, didn't he?'

A wave of sound rose up – then suddenly there wasn't a whisper.

Bannister swung up onto his feet.

'Objection!' he shouted.

'I should think the defense counsel *would* object,' said Galloway, bringing laughter. 'The witness will please answer.'

Elsa looked at the judge appealingly.

'Is the question pertinent?' asked Ditchburne.

'It is very pertinent,' said Galloway. 'I want to know why she is protecting this boy.'

'How do you mean – protecting him?'

'By saying that he was back by eleven o'clock on the night of the murder! Now, Mrs Bannister, did he kiss you that night on the beach?'

Elsa looked wildly at Bannister, but there was no hope there. He said nothing.

'The witness may answer,' said the judge.

Elsa said then, almost eagerly:

'Yes!'

Bannister sagged in his chair.

'And that's why Laurence stayed, isn't it?'

'I don't know—'

'Well, *I* would have stayed,' said Galloway.

A laugh went up, but Galloway wasn't laughing himself. He went on:

'And that's why you lied about the time he was back, isn't it? You wanted to protect him!'

'No!' she said. 'He *was* back before eleven. I know – I looked at the clock.'

'Remember, you are under oath.'

'I still say he was back before eleven o'clock. You don't like the truth because it means he *couldn't* have been down at Wall Street the night Mr Grisby was murdered – and he wasn't!'

Galloway came close to her.

'Mrs Bannister,' he boomed, 'do you know the laws in this state against perjury?'

I gripped the chair with both hands and waited.

'Yes!' she flared.

'But you admit he kissed you the night before?'

'Yes – but it didn't mean anything.'

'It didn't mean anything! Looking at you, I leave that to the jury. But I would also like to bring out this point: Laurence Planter didn't have a cent, as the saying goes. Even though you had expressed a romantic interest, he knew that after all you considered him just a chauffeur. To hold your interest, he would need money – and when he saw Mr Grisby draw the money from the bank—'

'Objection!' shouted Bannister. 'The District Attorney's remarks are merely conjecture.'

'Perhaps,' said Galloway. 'And perhaps not.'

He looked at the jurors to make sure they'd got the reason for my staying – to hold Elsa's interest by getting the five thousand from Grisby that I'd seen him draw out of the bank. They had, all right.

'Well, thank you, Mrs Bannister,' said Galloway. 'Your witness, Mr Bannister.'

Elsa caught her breath. We looked at each other, my heart pounding.

Bannister went up to the witness stand slowly. He didn't seem to want to question Elsa, yet he thought he had to, I guess.

'You testified,' he said, 'that Laurence was about to leave on the night of August eleventh and that you advised him to stay. You testified further that in doing this you held out no promise of a possible increase in pay. You had no reason to believe, then, that he was dissatisfied with the amount he was receiving?'

'No, none whatsoever.'

'Then you are quite sure that money, or the lack of it, had nothing to do with his wanting to leave?'

'Yes. I'm sure that money had nothing to do with it.'

'Then you are equally sure that it had nothing to do with his decision to stay?'

'Why—'

She started to answer. No words came. I didn't know whether it was the heat or whether she figured Bannister suspected the kiss had meant more than she said and was getting too close for comfort. Whatever it was, her eyes suddenly filmed over and she slumped down in the chair.

I jumped up, but Bannister caught her.

'May it please the Court!' he said. 'The witness is in no condition to continue. I ask for an immediate adjournment.'

'Request granted,' said Judge Ditchburne. 'The Court stands adjourned until ten o'clock tomorrow morning.'

I watched them carry Elsa into the judge's chamber. She really had fainted.

A newspaper man behind me was talking about her.

'Wow!' he said. 'Imagine being chauffeur for a dame like that. And he wanted to go back to sea!'

'Well, he might have been dumb, but *she* wasn't, that's a cinch.'

'What do you mean?'

'Why, what else do you think she got him to stay for? Maybe that's why she fainted, she thought Bannister was on to it.'

'Well, I'll tell you one thing – if they burn him, I'm going after that job myself. Did you happen to notice her eyes?'

'Her eyes!'

They started to laugh, but stopped when I turned around.

'You've got her all wrong,' I said. I wanted to bust them, but the guard yanked me away.

'O.K.,' one said. 'You ought to know, if anybody does!'

'You bet I ought,' I said.

IV

All during the next day, and the next, Galloway trotted out one witness after another. Each made it look worse for me than the last.

Steve Crunch, the truck driver, made it seem that I'd been drunk the night of the murder or I would never have run into his truck – not with the red light showing.

The man who'd come up in a bathrobe on the beach the next moment after I'd fired the shot made a lot about that. He told about taking the gun away from me and repeated the remark I had made about shooting it off for a whim.

Grisby's doctor, who'd made the blood test, said it checked with the blood on the money I'd hidden, also the blood I'd tried to 'wash out' in the car. And I had been careful not to do too good a job, so that the stains *could* be analyzed!

Then Galloway brought out the bank guard. He said that he had noticed me particularly because I had seemed nervous.

He proved to everyone's satisfaction that I had stood and watched Grisby draw the five thousand out of the bank; Bannister couldn't shake his identification.

A lot of others followed – people I'd never seen before, but who had seen me, and remembered. All came up and took a crack at me.

When they'd all finished, Galloway gave a little nod to the jurors, like he was making them a present of the case, all tied up in silk ribbons. Then he looked at Judge Ditchburne.

'The People rest,' he said.

Just like that. Not a word about the gun in the car being different from the one used to kill Grisby. Not a word about how Grisby had happened to be down on Wall Street, dead and dry, when I'd left him on the beach or thrown him into the Sound (depending on which confession of mine they wanted to take seriously, if any). Not a word about how the speedboat could have got back to the pier.

'How come?' I asked Bannister.

'He'll bring it up in his summary. He wants to see first what I'm going to do.'

'Well,' I said, 'what are you going to do?'

'There isn't much I can do, except try to raise a reasonable doubt about your guilt. We went over that.'

'Yeah, I know. But how are you going to do that? That's what I'm wondering about.'

'Watch!' he said.

Galloway had reached his table and was waiting for Bannister to begin, smiling at the jury to show how pleased he was with himself. The smile seemed to say, 'Don't let him kid you. He's going to do his best, he's paid to, but he hasn't a chance if you don't let him kid you. The kid's guilty as hell and everyone knows it, even him.'

Bannister got up and faced the judge.

'Your Honor,' he said, 'I move that the case against the defendant be dismissed for lack of evidence.'

There was a gasp that started with Galloway and ran all around the courtroom to the judge.

'Denied,' he said shortly.

Bannister looked surprised. It must have been an act. Even I wasn't surprised. There was enough evidence to send me to the chair a dozen times over, and Bannister knew it.

The funny thing was – it you could call it funny – that Grisby had known all the tricks and had used them to build up the evidence against me. And now here was Bannister, his partner, asking the judge to throw the case out of court because of lack of evidence – fighting his head partner and not knowing it. Or did he know it?

Anyway, he hadn't got very far.

'Very well,' he said. 'May it please the Court – ladies and gentlemen of the jury. I shall attempt to prove that the case against my client is purely circumstantial, that there is certainly a reasonable doubt of his guilt, at least on the charge of wilful intent to murder, and that the only real charge against him can be one of accidental, or excusable, homicide. I call first upon the District Attorney for the fatal bullet.'

This was the bullet used to kill Grisby. Bannister took it and offered it in evidence as Defendant's Exhibit A. When it was tagged, he held it up before the jury. Then he put the ballistics expert on the stand and got him to admit that the fatal bullet had not been fired from the gun known to have been in my possession.

'Now,' he said, 'it is not the purpose of the defense to attempt to show that Laurence Planter, the defendant, did not shoot Lee Grisby. That is admitted. The purpose is to show that it was an accident and no more, in which case you, the jury, must return a verdict of 'Not Guilty.' You have just learned that the State does not even have the evidence of the gun that was used. How then can it prove that he shot Lee Grisby, let alone that he shot him purposely, with deliberate intent to rob, as the State contends? The truth is that it *cannot* prove it. It is simply accepting the statement of the defendant himself, made in his voluntary confession, that he *did* shoot him.'

Of course, when it came his turn, Galloway tore that all to pieces. He turned the missing gun business around to convince the jury that I had shot Grisby purposely, after deliberate advance planning, other-wise why the second gun? And where was this second gun? Could I – *would* I – produce it? Of course not. I had thrown it away, as any murderer would have, in either the swamp or the Sound. The accident idea, a trick to fool the jury, had come later, after I'd been caught. No, it was a clear case of premeditated murder, and the second gun only went to prove it. But this came later.

Bannister went on:

'And how does the State account for the fact that the body was found down on Wall Street? The State's own witnesses, by their sworn testimony, have proved that it would have been absolutely impossible for the defendant to have taken the body there in the speedboat and then have returned the same way. Yet they do not say a word about that, and why? Because they know that there wasn't time for the round trip – *and the boat was tied up at the pier on my beach.*'

He brought out witnesses to tell how long it took to make the trip – at least a half hour each way on a dark night, and only an expert could do it. Galloway just turned that around, too, and made things worse for me than ever. He used McCracken's idea, that I had left Grisby for dead on the beach, and that he had then taken himself down to Wall Street in the speedboat. (How it got back didn't matter, he said, because the police didn't even look to see if it was at the pier until after two the next morning, plenty of time for me to have brought it back *after* Mrs Bannister had seen me at the garage at eleven, provided she was telling the truth.) And what he planted in the minds of the jury was the idea of my leaving a man to bleed to death on the beach *without any effort to help him.*

'Doesn't that show intent? Doesn't it show a vicious cruelty of mind, the sort of cold-blooded nature necessary to have planned this thing, planned it in all its grisly details, for the sake of a paltry five thousand dollars?'

This, like the gun business, came in Galloway's summary. Right now Bannister was closing his case. He was giving the jury a long-winded talk that sounded good but that said nothing, except that they should put themselves in my place. Small chance!

I turned around to look at Elsa. Everything else faded away, and I knew that it did for her too. And all at once tears came to her eyes.

I turned around just as Bannister said suddenly:

'The defense rests!'

For a second there wasn't a sound. Then Bannister came clumping back to the table and the whole courtroom began to buzz.

Galloway jumped up. He faced Judge Ditchburne.

'Your Honor,' he said, 'ladies and gentlemen of the jury. You have heard the evidence. It is conclusive. Nothing the defense counsel has said has changed the true course of that testimony one iota. Let's take his points one by one.'

This is where he began to tear down everything that Bannister had said, turning it all against me. It didn't take long. And then he went to the table where the exhibits were and snatched up the cap. He brought it over to the railing that ran in front of the jury box. He leaned on the railing and talked to each of the jurors in turn.

'The defense will have you believe that the shooting of Lee Grisby was an accident. Their whole defense is based on that plea. They say that we have only circumstantial evidence to support our contention that, far from being an accident, the shooting was murder committed in cold blood. Of course we have only circumstantial evidence with which to prove this. Ninety-nine murder cases out of a hundred are based on the same sort of evidence. How could it be otherwise? People don't go around committing murder under the eyes of the police. Yet should they be allowed to go free, to murder again, because no one saw the actual firing of the shot? The defense knows better – and even if it doesn't, the *jury* knows better.'

He stopped and held up the cap so that everyone could see.

'But even disregarding the sworn testimony of witnesses,' he went on, 'here is a *silent* witness – yet one that tells all you need to know.

Ladies and gentlemen, here is *positive proof* that the shooting of Lee Grisby was murder wilfully committed.'

What was all this? Even the judge looked interested.

'Because,' Galloway shouted, 'if the shooting had been an accident, *Grisby would not have been carrying this cap*. He would have had no reason to carry it. His keen legal mind would have been thinking of *sparing* this young man, not of *incriminating* him. Yet see him stagger from the scene, knowing himself mortally wounded. See him, even so, clutching in his last death throes to the one piece of evidence that he knew was certain to tell its story to the world – the grim, silent proof that he was murdered, the grim, silent *proof* of who that murderer was, the cringing, white-faced killer that sits before you now, *Laurence Planter!*'

I jumped as though I'd been shot out of the electric chair itself.

'Wait!' I yelled. 'I—'

The judge banged his gavel. At the same time Bannister grabbed me by the arm and tried to pull me back down into the chair.

'Sit down, you fool,' he said. 'Sit down! At least you've a chance now. Don't spoil it.'

I shook him off.

Judge Ditchburne glared at me.

'The defendant will please—'

'Listen!' I said above the noise.

The guard yanked me down into the seat. He held one arm, Bannister the other.

The judge kept rapping for order.

'Am I to understand that the defendant wishes to make a statement?'

I was trying to get up.

'Yes!' I yelled.

'I think if defense counsel had deemed it in your best interests to testify in your own behalf, he would have placed you on the stand at the proper time. As it is—'

'I don't care what he thought,' I said. 'All I want is the chance—'

'Very well, then, if counselor wishes, I shall grant a brief recess for discussion. I should only like to say to the defendant that Mr Bannister has conducted the case very ably up to this point, under the circumstances, and should advise against jeopardizing the case by too hasty action. If you wish, you can discuss the matter in my chambers.'

'Thank you, Your Honor,' said Bannister. He looked at me and scowled.

v

We filed into the judge's chambers and stood looking at each other. Bannister was so mad his nose was twitching.

The judge went over to a red leather couch and settled himself for a nap.

'Take your time,' he said. 'I don't want you to do anything you'll regret.'

He went to sleep.

'Now what?' asked Bannister. 'I told you why I didn't want to put you on the stand. It will just be playing into Galloway's hands!'

'Listen,' I said. 'You've been swell. No one could have done better. But if the jury goes out now, the way things are, they'll send me to the chair sure. And what else can I do but tell them what really happened?'

'Well,' he said, 'what really did happen?'

'I told you – Grisby wanted to get away from his wife. He took this way of doing it.'

'They'll never believe it. You follow my advice and stick to your story that it was an accident.'

'Supposing I don't?'

'Then I'm through with the case – right now.'

Elsa came in. She looked worried – plenty.

'Are you sure you ought to take the stand?' she asked me.

'It's my only chance.'

'Well, he's not going to do it so long as I'm defense counsel,' said Bannister. 'Not with any story about Grisby's wife. Galloway knows he didn't have a wife. He'd make chumps of us.'

'But it's his life,' said Elsa. 'If he feels he must talk, it's his right. Only—'

'It's his right,' said Bannister, 'but if he does, I'm through. And it's the end of him – they'll convict him sure.'

'No,' I said. 'Not when I get through talking.'

Bannister started for the door. Then he stopped and turned around.

'By what wild reasoning do you arrive at such a conclusion?' he asked. He shook his head sadly. 'No, I'll have the Court appoint a lawyer for you. If he wants you to talk – fine. But I'm through.'

'Marco—' said Elsa. 'Please—'

'He'll stay,' I said. 'He'll stay because I'm going to tell the jury just what happened – just who killed Grisby, and why. I was stalling when I said I'd tell them about Grisby's wife. What I'm going to tell them now will be the truth.'

'Now you're talking like a child. Come, Elsa.'

'All right,' I said. 'But if you leave it'll look as though you didn't want me to tell them – and for a good reason.'

'Yes?'

'Yes – that you killed Grisby!'

Bannister's mouth dropped open. Elsa stared first at him, then at me. She wasn't surprised, just frightened.

'You mean,' he said, 'that you'd actually get up there and tell such a preposterous – why, we talked that over before; I showed you then how absurd it was. You'd be laughed right out of court.'

'That would be fine,' I said. 'Anyway, I'm going to see.'

Bannister thought for a moment, pulling his nose. Then he shrugged.

'All right,' he said. 'But I warned you.'

The judge snored and woke up.

'Let's go,' I said.

Going out behind Bannister, Elsa squeezed my hand.

'I know it will work out all right,' she said. 'I know it will!'

I was sworn in and took the stand.

'Defendant may proceed,' said Judge Ditchburne.

I told them everything, just as I'd spilled my guts to Bannister in the letter I'd written, and which I'd later torn up. I said that he must have seen that letter, and that he must have laid for Grisby—

When I'd got that far, the courtroom began to buzz. The judge looked over at me and banged his gavel as though it was me he was hitting.

'Am I to understand,' he asked angrily, 'that you are confessing to having been in a murder plot against *your own lawyer?*'

'Yes. Except that I didn't want to do it. I had to. Grisby said he'd kill me if I didn't!'

'Am I to understand further,' he said, 'that you are accusing him now of having killed Lee Grisby *himself?*'

I got half way out of the chair.

'YES!' I said. 'BANNISTER KILLED GRISBY! That's what I wanted to tell you.'

The courtroom was in an uproar now. Everyone looked at Bannister. He just sat there, cool as could be.

The judge banged for silence. I went on:

'He said that the jury wouldn't believe it if I told them that I hadn't shot Grisby. He said our only chance was to pretend that I had shot him, and that it was an accident. Well, I didn't shoot him – not with the gun in the car or with any other gun. I didn't shoot him at all. He left of his own accord. He took that boat down to Wall Street himself – to kill Bannister. No one would think he had done it if he was supposed to be dead *himself* – that was the idea. But he'd no sooner got down to Wall Street than Bannister killed him.'

I was excited, but so was everyone else, even the judge. He looked over at Bannister almost apologetically.

Bannister stood up. He wasn't a bit flustered. He smiled at Judge Ditchburne and then looked over at Galloway.

'May it please the Court—'

Galloway was on his feet, too.

'But this it outrageous,' he said. 'It's obviously a last-minute grasping at straws. I ask Your Honor to disregard—'

'Your Honor,' said Bannister, 'I ask that the defendant be allowed to continue, that the jury may have no doubt that every right has been extended him.'

'Very well,' boomed Judge Ditchburne. He talked as though I'd been accusing *him*. 'The defendant may proceed.'

'I see now,' I went on, 'why Bannister advised me to plead guilty and to stick to the accident story. It was to protect himself. The police had looked into the chance that he might have done it and had given him a clean bill of health. That was swell – it was perfect. He didn't want them looking any further, if that's what they thought. He didn't want them finding out about the rear door of the building where he and Grisby had their offices. What Grisby had done was to unlock this door, so he could get back in at Bannister without the night watchman knowing. Usually it was kept locked.

'All right. Bannister knew what Grisby was going to do. After he left, he went out the rear door himself and waited down at the Skyport for Grisby to show up. Then he killed him, firing the shot from about the same angle it would have been fired if I had killed him accidentally in the car, so that it would all work against me. He knew from my letter that I was going to be suspected, if I went through with it. And he knew from the cap in Grisby's hand that I *had* gone through with it. Grisby had taken it to leave at the scene, so I'd be suspected of having killed Bannister. Then I'd show that I couldn't have killed Bannister by telling about killing Grisby. That would establish Grisby's death, and prove that *he* couldn't have killed Bannister – not if he was dead himself at about the same time, twenty miles away.

'The police say they looked into it – the chance that Bannister might have killed him, I mean. But did they? What alibi has he? Just that he was in his office when the watchman called to tell about Grisby, and that the watchman hadn't seen him go out of the building before that time. Sure he was there when the watchman called him. He had plenty of time before Grisby was found lying in the street. And sure, the rear door was locked when the police looked at it – do you think he would forget to *lock* it when he came into the building after killing Grisby? He'd thought of everything else.'

Judge Ditchburne leaned forward, his face redder than ever.

'Have you any proof of all this?' he asked. 'If you have not—'

I blazed up.

'Of course I haven't any proof,' I said. 'Nine-tenths of the murders committed are done without witnesses. If there were witnesses, they wouldn't be done. Ask Galloway. I'm just saying that the case against Bannister is stronger than the case against me. Bannister says that no jury can convict you if there is a reasonable doubt of guilt. I'm showing that there is a reasonable doubt of my guilt – and that Bannister had every reason to kill Grisby and that I had none, unless it was an accident, and I'm telling you that it wasn't, because I didn't shoot him at all.'

Galloway smiled and came up to me.

'If Your Honor please, I should like to ask the defendant a question.'

'Surely.'

'Why would Mr Grisby want to kill Mr Bannister – can you tell us that?'

'I didn't ask him. But he said he was going to get a lot of money out of it – and they had one hundred thousand dollars' worth of insurance between them – partnership insurance.'

'But if Grisby was supposed to be dead, too, how could he expect to collect this insurance?'

'I don't know,' I said.

'But speaking of money, *you* were going to get a large sum, too – and *you got it*. Five thousand dollars!'

'He gave it to me! I didn't take it!'

'But you hid it under your mattress, didn't you?'

'Yes, but—'

'That's all.'

So here was Galloway standing up for Bannister – that was a fine one!

'Listen!' I said. 'All that about why Grisby did what he did, and how Bannister beat him to it, is for you and the police to figure out. I'm just telling you the way it must have happened, because *I* didn't do it, and if I didn't do it, who could have? Only Bannister, because he'd be the only other person, outside of Broome and myself, who could have known about Grisby's plan to kill him. That's why he killed Broome – to keep him from talking. Broome must have seen the letter I'd left before I took Mrs Bannister out for the ride. That must have been how Bannister found out about what Grisby planned to do – Broome told him. So if Bannister killed Grisby, he'd have to kill Broome too, wouldn't he? If he didn't, as soon as the murder came out, Broome would tell the police that he must have beat Grisby to it.

'Well, *could* Bannister have killed Broome? He could have easily. He was with the police when they came out to the house to get me. I got scared and started to go out the window. Broome saw me and I had to knock him out to keep him from stopping me. I hit him, sure, but there wasn't time to choke him. But the police chasing me gave Bannister time to choke him. Maybe he wouldn't have, except that it was so easy to do. With Broome knocked out, why should he take a chance on his talking?'

Galloway popped up again.

'Your Honor,' he said, 'we are not considering here the murder of the detective Broome. I think—'

'Defendant will please confine his remarks to the case of Lee Grisby,' said the judge.

'And defendant will please remember also,' Galloway added, 'that it is he who is on trial for the murder of Lee Grisby, not his attorney.'

I looked at the jurors. They turned away, one after the other. For some reason they seemed to resent my accusing Bannister. That made me boil.

'Listen!' I said. 'I didn't kill Grisby. I didn't shoot him at all. I've told you the *truth*—'

They looked at me and through me.

I gave it up.

'That's all,' I said. 'Except – except—'

I started to choke up. I couldn't say another word. I climbed down off the stand and went over and sat beside Bannister.

'Well, you've done it now,' he said. 'The first case of this kind I've ever lost, too.'

He didn't seem to have the slightest feeling against me either for having entered into the plot against him or for accusing him in open court.

Galloway got up.

'May it please the Court, I have a few closing remarks to make to the jury.'

The judge nodded.

'The integrity of defense counsel is unquestioned,' said Galloway. 'The police and the Coroner's office and the Grand Jury each made a thorough investigation of all angles before preferring charges against the defendant. I think you may safely catalogue his remarks, therefore, as a desperate last-minute clutching at straws and render a verdict of guilty with all equanimity.'

'Then I am to understand,' said the judge, 'that in spite of the defendant's remarks, the District Attorney does not wish a warrant to be issued—'

'Absolutely not,' said Galloway. 'The State closes its case.'

Judge Ditchburne looked relieved.

'Very well, then,' he said. 'I have no other alternative than to instruct the jury to retire and to deliver a verdict based upon the facts as you know them. I need only add—'

And he went on to tell the jury exactly what verdicts were possible.

The jurors almost walked over each other trying to get out.

'So you think they'll convict me,' I said to Bannister.

'I'm sure of it. The very fact that you admitted to being in a murder plot against me, even if you were to be miles away at the time, and were entirely innocent of any actual wrong, is enough to send you to the chair. I told you that.'

He began to file his papers away, leaving me alone. I looked around. Elsa was sitting with her head down. Everyone else was talking and laughing.

VI

The jury came in before I was ready. They had been out only eighteen minutes.

My heart was beating so fast it shook me. My eyes were fogged over. Whatever happened, I didn't want to show it.

A sudden tense silence fell over the room, in which only the sound of Bannister's tapping on the table with his fingers could be heard.

I wasn't ready. My hands and face were streaming wet. I looked around to where Elsa had been sitting. She wasn't there. Then I saw her, close behind me. She smiled. I turned away and then back. She wasn't smiling at all. She was crying. Or maybe it was just the fog I saw her through this time. One minute everything would be clear, the next walls, ceiling, benches, people, all would be swimming together.

The clerk stepped forward. He had a military haircut and snapped out his words.

'The jury will stand.'

They stood.

'Have you agreed upon a verdict?'

The foreman cleared his throat.

'We have,' he said.

The clerk looked over at me like a ringmaster cracking his whip.

'Prisoner, stand up!'

I stood up. It was like being in a sinking elevator. I lurched and held onto the table. As my hand came down, Bannister jerked his back.

'The jury will look upon the prisoner. The prisoner will look upon the jury. How say you: Guilty or Not Guilty?'

I saw the foreman say the word before I heard the sound – like they say you feel the bullet before you hear the shot:

'Guilty!'

The formal sentence came later. They brought me through the same steel-barred door and stood me before the judge – not Ditchburne this time.

'Laurence Planter,' he said, 'you have been convicted of the slaying of Lee Grisby, and it is my duty now to pass sentence upon you.'

'Yes, sir,' I said. 'Only I'm not guilty. I didn't kill him, accidentally or any other way. It's just like I said—'

I looked around the courtroom. *Someone* must believe me. But there were only a few people sitting around. They hardly looked up at all. One man was even eating his lunch.

The judge went on as though he hadn't heard me, either.

'It is the sentence of this court that you be taken hence to Sing

Sing Prison and placed there in confinement, and that, during the week of February the sixth, you shall be put to death in the manner prescribed by the laws of this state.'

My mouth dropped open.

'Listen!' I said. 'I—'

The judge turned to the clerk.

'Next case!'

Back in the cell, the words kept pounding over and over in my head, each time louder even than when he had said them:

'. . . THAT, DURING THE WEEK OF FEBRUARY THE SIXTH, YOU SHALL BE PUT TO DEATH IN THE MANNER PRESCRIBED BY THE LAWS OF THIS STATE.'

Me – me!

And I had never even killed a rat, or winged a bird . . .

PART FIVE

I

February eighth – the death cell!

Thirty-three hours, twenty-two minutes, fifteen seconds to go.

The executions were set for Thursday night at eleven o'clock. Two others were slated to go with me. Who would be first down the 'dance hall' none of us knew. Probably me. I hadn't broken – yet.

Only the Governor could stop it now. Or a confession by the one who really did kill Grisby. Because *I* didn't kill him, you know I didn't. Everyone else was figuring that I did. Everyone but Elsa.

Even the judge who did the sentencing said it wasn't right. He didn't say I was innocent, just that it wasn't right. The reason he'd barked out, 'Next case!' was because there wasn't anything he could do about it. The papers told what he really thought the next day . . . maybe you read it:

Following his formal sentencing of Laurence Planter to death yesterday, Judge O'Connell delivered a surprising comment on the value to society of the death penalty. His views are certain to provoke widespread comment. Judge O'Connell spoke as follows:

'In passing upon the verdict and the penalty, the court finds its public duty in conflict with its private conscience. There are many survivals of the barbaric and the medieval that at times belie the advance of civilization.

'The life-for-a-life philosophy is a relic of feudalism. We have discovered no ideal crime-free state where the corrosive passions of jealousy, envy, hate and the attendant evils are non-existent. That a debt to society can be paid by a human body put to death is a philosophy incrusted with social futility.

'The verdict of capital punishment for Laurence Planter, in a case filled still with mysteries unsolved and whole curious phases still unexplored, has incited an equally divided opinion of its severity as well as its fitness. But it is the law of this state that the only avenue of clemency open to the defendant in addition to appeal is vested by law in the chief executive of the state, who is empowered to commute the sentence or even to pardon.'

Bannister was seeing the Governor now. Would he get the pardon? And did he *want* to?

Judge O'Connell had been careful to keep Bannister in the clear. He said he had conducted the trial 'commendably, in a legal and ethical manner.'

Sure he had – why not? He'd known all along what the verdict would be. The case against me was so strong, he hadn't needed to pull his punches to make sure they'd convict me.

Or did I have him wrong? Maybe he hadn't killed Grisby after all – or Broome. Maybe I *had* just been clutching at straws when I said he'd done it.

But I didn't believe it. I'd been clutching at straws, maybe – who wouldn't? But they were the right straws, I was positive. Only – how could I prove it?

Three o'clock.

Everything was ready. All except me.

I began to sweat, shivering.

Why didn't he come? I had the same panicky feeling I had waiting for the police to come the night I'd 'killed' Grisby. Only then I'd run away, out into the swamp.

Now I couldn't run away.

'Most people live only when they are about to die.'

It was funny. I hadn't paid much attention to Bannister, the night he'd been spouting on the beach. He'd been drunk, I guess that was why. But there wasn't anything he had said that I'd forgotten, I found now.

And the next night on the beach, with Elsa. If what he had said about 'seizing the moment' hadn't sunk in a little – more than I had thought – I might never have made love to her, and then this never would have happened. Because I wouldn't have stayed on, no matter what threats Grisby made if I didn't go through with it.

I wouldn't be *awake*, either. Not that it mattered much now. They were going to kill me just as I started to live. Like Bannister – remember? – telling about what had made him bitter:

'Bitter!' he'd said to the waves. 'They wonder why I am bitter . . . Because, awakened, I was eager to grasp the fruits of life before it was too late. And reaching out for them – what happened? A shell, a burst of red – the whole sky whirling red – blackness – a twisted leg – the fruits denied.'

But at least they hadn't *killed* him just as he woke up. There was still a chance he might do something about it, in spite of his leg. After you're dead, it doesn't make much difference whether you are awake or asleep. Or maybe I was getting bitter too.

All I knew was, if they killed me now, my life would be over almost before it had begun.

II

It is an unwritten code in Sing Sing that during the week before an execution all other condemned will give up their visiting privileges in favor of those about to die.

There was someone to see me.

I was led out to one of the three visiting cells. Before me, behind a heavy steel mesh screen, stood Sergeant McCracken.

'I just dropped in to see how you were,' he said. 'I'm down here on official business. How are you?'

'Fine,' I said, 'but it's lucky you found me in.'

'I know. Tough. If there were only more time . . .'

'What do you mean?'

'I mean if there were more time I might get you out. The more I think about it, the more it seems you didn't do it.'

'This is a swell time to tell me.'

'Oh, I've been working on the case, don't think I haven't. What started me was the way you accused Bannister in court, when you told about the "false murder." But it's a tough case to crack, all right. I haven't been able to find any new evidence yet that would make the Governor put the execution off. If Bannister did the killing he's covered his tracks at every turn.'

'Maybe he hired someone else to do it, then.'

'No, he'd be too smart to take a risk like that. Besides, he didn't make any withdrawals from the bank that would account for that.'

'Then the only chance is if he confesses?'

'If! There isn't much chance of that. Why should he confess if he did it? You even admitted being in the plot against him. He should worry about you. No, the only chance is if some new evidence turns up, like the gun used in the killing. But I'll do everything I can. I'll put a tail on him. I'll watch every scrap of mail. I'll work on it right up to the—'

'Thanks,' I said. 'Bannister's seeing the Governor now. Maybe—'

'I know. I just saw the Warden. He's keeping the wires open to Albany. I'll let you know the minute anything breaks.'

But I could tell he didn't think there was much hope.

III

There was a rat in the cell with me.

Suddenly the hair on my neck bristled, I did not know why. I looked up startled, and there he was, crouched in a corner. It was a question who was the most surprised.

We did not move.

The light was weak; already the sky was bedding down for the night. Far away a train whistle sounded, a lonely, hurt wail.

I remembered the rats in the swamp. This one's eyes seemed almost human.

We sat and waited.

The whistle faded . . . somewhere people were happy, free, going to new places, new sounds. The whistle died.

Still we did not move.

Off in another cell a man was crying. He said over and over, under his breath, 'Oh, my God . . . Oh, my God . . .' He was one of the three slated to go down the 'dance hall' to the chair tomorrow night. He poisoned his wife in a suicide pact – then forgot to take some himself.

I was one of the three, too – and I had killed no one.

I seized the stool; the rat dived under the bunk. I yelled at him to come out and fight. He darted toward the door.

But I was quicker. I came down hard with the stool. It caught him on the side, just as he reached the bars. He dragged himself on, stunned but still fighting. I grabbed him by the tail.

Now – now!

I swung him around my head. He curved back to bite my hand. I smashed his head against the wall.

Blood and brains splattered.

He was dead.

IV

At last!

Bannister came in. His dark hawk's face was blacker than ever, but his eyes were bright, burning. Without smelling the Scotch on his breath I could see that he had been hitting it strong.

I wet my lips.

'You saw the Governor?'

'Yes – I saw him.'

'No luck?'

'No luck.'

We stared at each other.

'Then it's all over?'

He shrugged.

'I did all I could – more than anyone else could have, under the circumstances. After all, you made love to my wife, didn't you? You helped Grisby plot the perfect crime against me, didn't you? And then, when it failed, you accused me of his murder, didn't you? Do you think anyone else would have helped you as much as I have?'

I could feel the hot blood rush to my head.

'You'd have to have a damned good reason, you're right. And you did have – the best reason of all – that you killed him yourself! You took the case to make sure I didn't get off.'

He smiled.

'There never was much doubt about the verdict, especially after you went against my judgment and admitted being in a plot with him. Whether they believed it or not, it was still bad. You ought to see that now.'

I was boiling mad.

'I don't see it at all. I didn't kill him – you did, you did! Why don't you confess? Why let me go to the chair for something you did yourself? They'd never send *you* to the chair. All you have to do is plead self-defense. He was going to kill you – I can prove it! It's a perfect case of self-defense.'

He shook his head.

'No – that's where you don't know the law. Oh, of course, if a man walks up to you and threatens your life with a homicidal instrument, you are entirely within your rights of self-defense to kill him. But if you have fair warning, if you know that he is coming to take your life and you lay a trap for him, then you are as guilty as he would be, even though that would be by far the more sensible course.'

'And that's what you did.'

'I didn't say that.' He laughed. 'Though I will say, it would have been poetic justice if I had. I'll give Grisby credit – he *planned* the perfect crime. I'd like to think he made one fatal mistake – he underestimated his man. Instead of being the *victim* of the perfect crime, I committed it! The perfect crime reversed! But, I'm sorry – I can't say that.'

'You can't because you won't.'

I turned wildly to look for the guards. The man in the cell down the way – the one who'd been crying all afternoon, 'Oh, my God, oh, my God' – was yelling like a madman, bringing the guards on the run.

'Get me out of here,' he shrieked. 'I can't stand it. I'll go crazy. I'll slam my head against the wall.'

The guards were trying to quiet him.

Bannister smiled.

'Maybe he's seen an execution before,' he said. 'Have you? I'll tell you about it. Tomorrow morning they'll put you in a pre-execution cell. They'll give you a big dinner, anything you want. Then along about eleven tomorrow night – they used to have the executions at five in the morning, but this makes it more cozy – the guards will come in and slit your right trouser leg. That's so they can fit the electrode on when they strap you in the chair. Then they'll lead you down a little corridor, if you can walk; if not, they'll carry you. You'll go into the execution chamber and up to a large square chair—'

'Guard!'

'One man will hold your arms, another your legs. In a minute the straps will be adjusted, a hood will go down over your head – but before it drops, you'll—'

'Guard!'

My voice was so low and hoarse they did not hear. Bannister smiled.

'It won't do you any good to call the guards. Besides, you ought to be grateful to me, if you really think I killed him. I might have killed you, too, as you say I did Grisby and Broome.'

'But why? What did *I* do?'

'You were in the plot against me, weren't you? Isn't that enough? It's too bad about you in a way, I'll admit – you were just a tool. At least there's some merit in your case; all you were to do was to pretend to kill someone. Besides, Grisby threatened to kill you if you didn't go through with it. It wasn't as though you wanted to.'

'That ought to let me out, oughtn't it? Besides, if I hadn't written that letter telling you what he planned to do, you'd never have known about it – he'd have got you sure!'

'Yes – but I never received the letter. You tore it up. If Broome saw it first, as you said at the trial, he didn't tell me. Anyway, what you should have done was come to me directly. If you had done that, instead of doing just what they told you to, you wouldn't be worrying about going to the chair now. You'd be as free to walk out as I am.'

'Except that then you'd have had to kill me, too, like you did Broome!'

'You forget that the plan would have fallen through if you had refused to do what they said. As it happened, it fell through anyway, but it wasn't your fault that Grisby got killed. Or was it?'

I got it this time. I started to tingle all over.

'"They"? What do you mean – *"they"*? There was only Grisby!'

He stood back and looked at me with his face working in surprise. 'Only Grisby!' he said.

'Why, sure. You didn't think – *Broome?*'

Still he looked at me. Then he shook his head slowly, almost sadly.

'I knew you were dumb,' he said, 'but I didn't think you were *that* dumb.'

My temples began to throb. I ran a hand over my forehead. It came away wet.

I could hardly talk.

'You mean – your *wife?*' I whispered.

'Why, certainly! She and Grisby planned it together, the whole thing.'

I nearly dropped through the floor.

Grisby and Elsa!

I tried to catch my breath. Nothing seemed real any more. Bannister was just a vague blur. But I could hear him still. His voice came as through a fog:

'That's why I put Broome out there – I knew something was up between them. Well, well. They were clever, all right – you never even guessed it. But *I* did . . .'

I began to remember things.

I remembered Grisby talking to me about Bannister, 'He's all washed up and doesn't know it.'

I remembered Elsa – Elsa saying to Bannister, 'Has it honestly never occurred to you that you might be better off dead?'

Grisby and Elsa!

And the night on the beach, when she stopped me from leaving. Pretending to be in love with me – why? Just so I'd go through with my part! I saw it all now.

'Tomorrow!' she whispered.

A promise . . .

Tomorrow I'll go to the chair . . . because of her. Tomorrow!

I remembered other things now, too. Something she'd said once when she came to see me before the trial.

'I had to come, I had to! I feel somehow – somehow as though I were responsible for your being here.'

Crying while she'd said it – crying often afterwards. Because I was in jail – or because Bannister had turned the tables and killed Grisby? She must have known all along that Bannister had done it – *she must have!*

And Broome – the way he'd talked about her and about Grisby:

'You don't think he comes out here just to see *Bannister*, do you?'

'You've got her all wrong,' I'd said. And believed it! Believed it all the way up to now!

Bannister laughed, I looked so stunned. It brought me back to earth.

He said: 'Why do you suppose Grisby wanted to kill me, if not because of her? Hadn't you thought about that at *all?*'

My mouth was so dry I could hardly talk.

'He said it was to – to get a lot of money.'

'He told you about the partnership insurance between us?'

'No – I found out about that later. I thought that's what he must have meant.'

'But didn't you see how absurd that was? How could he collect if he was supposed to be dead himself? He couldn't! The only way he could hope to get it was through Elsa. She'd inherit everything – and get the partnership insurance, too, if both Grisby and I could be proved dead. That's why your part was so important – that and to throw suspicion off himself for my murder. Of course, all this is just guess-work, but how else could he get the money but through Elsa?'

Elsa! I couldn't believe it!

'Oh, it was the perfect crime,' Bannister went on. 'I'll give them credit there, at least if they planned it the way I think they did now. That's why I said it's too bad about you going to the chair for it – you were just the tool.'

Suddenly it didn't make much difference about going to the chair any more. Elsa—

Now Bannister seemed to be talking far away. I could hardly hear him:

'Of course, Broome knew about Grisby and Elsa. That's why he was there – to keep an eye on them. He didn't know about the plan to kill me – at least he didn't that I know of – and certainly I didn't know it either. But he was keeping close watch, and he did know that they planned to run away together. The night before you were going to fake Grisby's "murder" – when Grisby came out to have dinner with us – what do you suppose he was doing when I left him alone with Elsa, with Broome listening? *Arguing about the South Seas –* whether Tahiti was the best place! Broome heard it all outside the window; he told me right after.'

So Elsa was going to meet Grisby in the South Seas! I had been dumb, all right. She must have laughed plenty – me thinking she was in love with me, when it was Grisby all the time.

'Well,' I said, 'you got Grisby. Why didn't you get her, too?'

The question startled him. He breathed liquor into my face.

'*Kill my wife?* That would be killing *me.* If anything happened to her – if I lost her – what would I have to live for? She's life, youth, everything that otherwise would be denied me . . .'

The guard looked in at us.

'Hey, guard!' I yelled. 'I've been trying to get you. Bannister practically told me he killed Grisby – to keep him from running away with his wife!'

'Oh, yeah?'

'Call the Warden. Hold him till he comes!'

Bannister laughed.

'He's hysterical,' he said. 'Well, I did all I could for you. Laurence. No one could have done more. The cards were just stacked against you, I guess.'

'Yes – and you stacked them!'

'Better let him alone,' said the guard. 'He's only working himself up.'

Bannister nodded.

'Well, good-bye, then,' he said.

I was so choked up I couldn't say a word. I just stood and watched him go out – my last chance to beat the chair, as I figured it. Even the way he walked, with that funny jerky stride, seemed to be mocking me.

Back in the cell, I threw myself down on the bunk and cried like a baby.

Elsa! Elsa and Grisby!

It didn't seem possible . . .

I heard the guard calling my name.

'What's the matter with you? This is the third time I've called. There's someone to see you.'

I tried not to sound as though I had been crying.

'I guess I didn't hear.'

'Well, get a move on.'

I followed him out to the visiting cell – and nearly dropped. Beyond the screen was – *Elsa!*

V

I stared at her.

She raised her veil. Her face was white.

'I saw him!' she said. 'I think he saw me, too! It was just as I was coming in. He was getting into a cab. I didn't look back. How awful, if he should find me here. But I had to come – I had to see you. Laurence—'

I couldn't talk. I just looked at her.

She backed away.

'Why – why do you stare at me like that? Has something happened?'

I looked down at the floor. My body sagged. She thought it was because I had given up.

'Oh, Laurence – There must be some way out, there must be!'

I looked up at her again.

'No . . . I'm done for.'

Her eyes moved back and forth over mine. All at once tears rolled down her cheeks.

'I love you so much,' she said.

I found my voice. I blatted out:

'So much that you're sending me to the chair for something I didn't do. So much that you used me for a tool. If it hadn't been for you, I wouldn't be here. I'd be out at sea somewhere—'

It was just as though I had hit her.

She staggered back.

'Why, Laurence! You don't know what you're saying!'

'Oh, don't I! You and Grisby cooked up the whole thing – you let me make love to you so I'd stay on the job and go through with my part. You don't give a damn about me and never did. It was Grisby all the time. You were going to meet him down at Tahiti – I know all about it. Bannister told me everything. He got it all from Broome.'

'But – but that's *crazy!*'

'What did you do, come down here to gloat, like Bannister did? Well, you can get out – I've had enough. I'll go to the chair – I'll go and be glad of it.'

'Laurence – wait! Who told you this? It isn't true. Listen to me – you have to listen to me – it isn't true.'

'I listened to you once before and look what it got me.'

'But I can't have you go to your – to your death, with such thoughts. Don't you see? It isn't true – I—'

'You! Do you know what I'd do if I was out there? Yes, right now – this minute! I'd take that lily-white neck of yours in my hands—'

'Laurence!' she screamed. Her hands went to her throat.

'I'd choke you like Bannister choked Broome. I'd smash you against the wall like I did the rat in my cell. Then, at least, when they killed me it would be for a reason – not just because you let me make love to you one night on the beach. And you even held back on that!'

The tears were streaming down her face.

'Please, please, listen to me!'

'I suppose you weren't going to meet Grisby down in the South Seas . . . after he killed Bannister?'

She was silent.

'That's all I wanted to know.'

I turned and started to go out.

'Laurence, wait!'

Something in her voice made me stop.

'Grisby asked me to meet him there, yes. He'd been after me for months to go away with him. Is that what you mean?'

I shook my head.

'Not just that he asked you – that you said you'd go.'

'But I didn't!'

Now I had her.

'Broome heard you and Grisby arguing about it. That was the night before I drove him down to the beach. You must have said yes – it was that night he told me he had decided definitely to kill Bannister. Bannister beat him to it, that's all. But don't tell me you didn't know.'

'Please! He argued with me because I told him I couldn't do it – I couldn't meet him at Tahiti or anywhere. That's what Broome heard – only he couldn't have heard all of it. Because I said it would kill Marco for me to leave him. You don't understand what I mean to him – everything, his life!'

'So you fixed it with Grisby to get him out of the way.'

She moved over closer and leaned against the screen.

'Oh, how can you say that? I pitied him – I told Lee it was hopeless, to forget it, I couldn't leave Marco, I was too much a part of him. He asked me if it would be different if it weren't for Marco. I was unhappy, you know how unhappy I was. I said everything would be different. I didn't realize what he meant to do, or that he would think I *would* go with him if it weren't for Marco. But it made him so happy, I couldn't tell him the truth – that I didn't love him, it was impossible.'

I began to see that Bannister might have been all wrong about her. I saw, too, how Broome could have been on the wrong track, hearing little bits here and there.

'Listen!' I said. 'That may all be, but you must have known that Bannister was the one who killed Grisby – you must have! Yet you didn't say anything at the trial.'

'What could I say? That Marco killed him because of jealousy over me? Is that what you mean?'

'Partly.'

'But I couldn't say that. So far as I knew, Marco hadn't the slightest idea that Lee wanted me to leave him, or that he was paying me any particular attention. Of course, when I found out Broome was a detective, I was afraid. But even knowing that he had been watching me, even knowing how jealous Marco could be—'

She stopped biting her lip.

'So then he did kill him after all!' she said.

'Yes, and Broome, too! Nobody else *could* have!'

'And he would – he would let you go to the chair for something he had done himself? Why, he even defended you!'

'Yes – to make sure I'd go to the chair!' An idea came to me. 'You said that the only reason you stayed with him was because you pitied him. Do you still?'

She looked at me with her eyes flashing.

'No!'

'You said you loved me. Do you still?'

Her eyes softened.

'Yes!'

'All right, then. Prove it! Tell Bannister you're through. Tell him you know all about him killing Grisby – and Broome—'

'But we don't know that – not for sure.'

'This will get him to confess. He'll crack, I know it.'

'It would kill him.'

'He's going to let me go to the chair in his place, isn't he? Will you do it?'

'I—'

And suddenly there he was – standing right behind her.

Bannister!

VI

Bannister grabbed her by the arm. His lips were white in a face dark with anger.

'What are you doing here?' he demanded.

He was so angry he shook her.

She tried to free herself. Bannister tightened his grip.

McCracken came in. He stopped with his mouth open.

'What the hell . . .'

Bannister paid no attention. His voice was sharp, bitter. It sent shivers all through me.

'A touching scene – the lovers parting in the shadow of the chair! And you said that kiss on the beach didn't mean anything! I suppose Grisby didn't mean anything, either!'

Elsa was cold. She did not struggle any more.

'Please – my arm—'

The way she said it made him drop back.

'You're not going to deny—'

'I don't deny anything. I love him.' Her voice rose. 'Are you going to deny that you killed Grisby – and Broome?'

He was ready for that.

'Of course I am! It's ridiculous. He's grasping at straws. He tried to do the same thing in court. Elsa – you don't believe—'

She just looked at him.

'Listen!' he said.

She said slowly, coldly, 'And you'd let an innocent man suffer for something you did yourself!'

'Elsa! Listen—'

Suddenly she tore into him. It was like a dam bursting, the way the words poured out.

'I'm through listening! I married you because of pity. I stayed with you for eight years – for eight years! Because I knew what it meant to you. Because you were always brooding about your leg and the things that were "denied" you. Nothing was denied you – it was all in your own twisted mind. Your warped, jealous mind! There wasn't a bit of truth about my going away with Lee. You imagined the whole thing – and you killed him! Now I'm going to the Governor. I'm going to tell him everything I know. If your own wife turns against you, it ought to mean something. At least it will stop them from killing an innocent man!'

Bannister came toward her.

'You can't leave me – you know you can't. You know it would kill me. I'd – I'd kill myself.'

Elsa didn't back down an inch.

'Isn't that exactly what you deserve, letting an innocent man go to the chair for you?'

McCracken and I looked on without saying a word. Silence clapped down on us – a humming silence like high tension wires about to snap.

Bannister looked shaken. You could tell that the liquor had fogged his brain.

'Elsa . . . please. This is ridiculous, the whole thing. Let's talk like civilized human beings.'

'There's nothing more to talk about – nothing at all, ever.'

Bannister moved his lips, but no words came. He seemed to be crumbling to pieces right before our eyes.

McCracken stepped up and shook him.

'What's this about your killing Grisby?'

Bannister paid no attention. He said to Elsa, almost in a whisper: 'Then you meant it – we're through?'

The whisper came back:

'It's over – everything. Even pity.'

Bannister saw there was no use talking here. He turned toward the door, lurching a little to one side, gasping when it hurt his leg. Trying to play on her pity! He expected her to call him back. When she didn't, he went on.

McCracken tried to stop him.

'What about this, did you kill him or didn't you?'

'He did!' I yelled. 'He as much as told me. He thought she was going to run away with him!'

Bannister didn't even hear. He went out half dazed.

'Follow him,' I said. 'Get him to confess!'

'I'll watch him every minute,' said McCracken. 'Don't worry.'

Elsa came over to the screen. Her eyes were gleaming.

'You were wonderful,' I said. 'Now maybe he'll confess.'

'I've only started,' she said. 'I'm going to the Governor. He'll have to believe me. He'll have to stop this before it's too late. Don't lose hope. I'll be thinking of you every minute. There must be something that can be done – there must be.'

She hurried out.

I went back to my cell to wait. Now everything would be fine, I hadn't a doubt of it. The Governor would give me the reprieve or Bannister would confess, one or the other. I didn't even try to sleep – I was too excited, waiting, waiting . . .

About midnight the Warden came in to see me.

'The Governor and I had a long talk,' he said. 'He told me that Mrs Bannister had come to plead for you on the ground that her husband had confessed. He made an immediate investigation.'

'That's swell.'

'Bannister denied everything. With no definite evidence to act on, the Governor was in a spot. He knew that you had accused Bannister once before, apparently without foundation. What could he do? What would *you* have done? I think the same thing he did – refuse to grant you a stay. He had no alternative, don't you see? I'm sorry, Laurence—'

So now there was only one hope left – for Bannister to confess. It was all up to him now.

After the Warden had left, I slipped out of the bunk and knelt down beside it. I knew only one prayer. I put everything I had into it:

> 'Now I lay me down to sleep,
> I pray the Lord my soul to keep;
> If I die before I wake . . .'

VII

February ninth!

This was the day . . . *six hours, twenty-two minutes, thirteen seconds to go!*

All I could think of was that by midnight the hands of the clock would have met like shears to snip another life, and this time mine.

Mine!

I paced the cell – and waited.

Suddenly the guard unlocked the door. He saw that I hadn't

touched the dinner they brought me. I told him to take it away, to give it to someone else. My last big meal!

'Okay,' he said, 'but get a move on. There's someone to see you.'

A visitor! It was almost like being freed. I hurried out.

It was Elsa.

For a while we did not speak. We just looked at each other; that was enough. Little by little a peace stole over me.

'Laurence—'

'Yes?'

'I saw the Governor.'

'The Warden told me. You were wonderful. If there had been any – any chance at all, you'd have got me off, I know.'

'Oh, there's still a chance. Don't think—'

'Sure. You never know until the last minute. They let one off just this morning, one of those who was going to go with me. He was always yelling, "Oh, my God!" He killed his wife.'

Her mouth trembled.

'You don't mean – the one in the *suicide pact!*'

'That's the one. He made out he was crazy. Maybe he was. He acted like it.'

But it didn't do any good. The fact remained that they were letting him off and he was guilty. I was innocent, yet they were sending me to the chair.

My throat tightened; an ache came to it.

'I know how you feel,' she said. 'I know – so well. Believe me, everything that is happening to you is happening to me too, deep down inside. I told you, if I hadn't stopped you, that night, you wouldn't be here. Oh, Laurence – I wish—'

'What?'

'I wish I could go with you!'

A surge went through me . . . a surge like great music rising. My blood sang. I felt light, as though I were floating. I thought: nothing can stop this. *Nothing!* No one has ever loved like this before. It can't end in my going to the chair. Something must happen to stop it. Bannister *must* confess.

'I'll get out,' I said. 'Something will happen, even if the Governor—'

'He has no proof, only your word. Don't you see? He can't stop it just because he *wants* to!'

'I know. It's all up to Bannister now. If he doesn't confess, now that you've left him – But he will. He *has* to!'

She put her hand to the screen to feel my hand pressing through.

'I saw him – this morning.'

'You did!'

'I had to. I had to get *proof*. He was the only one who could give it to me. I – I asked him to confess.'

'What did he say?'

'He laughed. It was awful. I think he had been drinking steadily, from the moment he left here. He said he hadn't slept all night. When I hadn't come home he'd realized what was happening. He knew then that I'd meant it and that this was the end. The house seemed so empty and still . . . he'd even frightened the maid away.'

She looked away from me and at the floor.

I did not dare say anything.

'He said I couldn't leave him. He said he'd built his whole life around me; if I left there'd be nothing to live for. But he said he knew I'd come back, too, that I couldn't leave him. I told him why I'd come – to get him to confess, that only by confessing to save an innocent man from the chair could he prove himself worthy of my staying with him. It was crazy, just like that. But he was so – well, so *unbalanced* that you couldn't talk any other way. And I think the main thing was he realized, underneath everything, that he'd killed Grisby without reason, that there'd been nothing between us at all except in his jealous mind.'

I started to tingle. Everything was working out the way I'd hoped when I'd asked her to prove that she loved me – by telling Bannister she was through. If he didn't confess now, with everything against him, he never would. I held my breath.

She went on:

'We talked for an hour. He kept repeating that I couldn't leave him – even if he killed himself, I couldn't. The way he said it made me afraid. He said I couldn't deny that there had been something between Grisby and me, that we had planned to meet in the South Seas –

Broome had heard it. He kept coming back to that to justify what he had done, even knowing that it wasn't true. Finally he admitted that he had killed Lee—'

This was it! Now he'd confess everything and I would go free!

'I asked him to put that on paper. He said to wait – he had just what was needed to fix everything. He went upstairs to the safe, I think – and came down with something in his hand behind him. He said he'd been saving it for just such an emergency as this. I asked him what it was, and then he brought it out – a revolver! He pointed it at me . . .'

'He was going to kill you!'

'Yes! . . . That's what he meant when he said I couldn't leave him. If he went, I would have to go, too. He raised the gun . . .'

I waited, breathless.

'He asked *me* to confess – to admit that I had had an affair with Lee, and with *you*. I told him he was crazy and to put down the gun. He came closer. I was terrified. I knew McCracken was near. I screamed for him. I saw him turn the gun on himself—'

'*What!*'

'Laurence – I didn't want to tell you, to destroy your last hope—'

I was weak.

'What – what do you mean – my last hope?'

'Laurence – *Marco is dead!*'

VIII

'Dead!'

I was stunned. I couldn't believe it. Bannister – *dead!*

She told me all about it. He was going to kill her. It was partly the drink, partly his crazed, jealous mind. But McCracken had been near. When she'd screamed for him, he'd come on the run.

Bannister had heard him coming. He'd thought only of himself – to stop McCracken from arresting him – what else? And he'd turned the gun on himself before McCracken could come in and stop him.

My lips quivered as I said it:

'So then – he didn't confess—'

'No. There wasn't time, even if he had wanted to.'

My voice shook: 'Then that's the end of me. There's nothing that can stop it now – nothing!'

'Oh, there's still hope! Believe me – I know I shouldn't have told you, though. I didn't mean to. I wanted you to think – maybe – even up to the last, even if what I hoped wasn't true—'

'But he killed himself! That's the same as a confession, isn't it?'

'I talked to Sergeant McCracken. He said no – I had left him, that was enough to make him kill himself, even without the other. He'd threatened to do it, you know – when I told him we were through. But it's the gun, Laurence – the gun! Sergeant McCracken is checking it now, to see if it's the same one used to kill Grisby. If it is—'

'Yes, and if it isn't—'

'Laurence, listen!'

We looked at each other until my eyes blurred over.

'What?'

'If it isn't,' she said, '—if it isn't, I meant what I said, about wishing I could go to the chair with you!'

'Well, that's fine,' said a voice behind us. 'Because it looks like you'll get your wish. Only you won't be going with anyone – you'll be going alone!'

Sergeant McCracken!

'What do you mean?' she said. 'You don't mean—'

'I mean I'm arresting you for the murder of Mark Bannister – and Grisby – and Broome!'

'Hey, watch her!' I yelled. 'She's going to faint.'

He caught her as she fell.

'Humm,' he said, 'I didn't think she had it in her.'

I was suddenly angry.

'What are you doing?' I yelled. 'Leave her alone! You're crazy if you think she killed anyone. What are you trying to do here?'

He looked at me with his mouth open.

'You mean you didn't even guess?' he said.

'Then it's true? She really—'

'No doubt about it. You'll be free within twenty-four hours – free!'

I was so stunned I could hardly think or talk. I kept staring at Elsa, lying in his arms, her face deathly white.

McCracken was rubbing her wrists.

'What a fool I've been,' he said. 'Talk about your perfect crime! She'd have got away with it, too, if it hadn't been for one thing. She forgot fingerprints on the gun Bannister was supposed to have killed himself with. Either forgot them or didn't have time to wipe them off, I came in so soon. It was Bannister's gun, all right, and it was the gun used to kill Grisby – she knew that, and she knew that we'd check it, too – not for fingerprints, it looked so much like suicide, but for bullets. Well, we did check it – and found her fingerprints on it! That was the one place she slipped up. Until then, we hadn't even suspected her. I don't mean we hadn't considered her as a possibility. It's just that she didn't fit in anywhere, even if we figured your story was true about Grisby trying to kill Bannister, and went a step further and had her in it with Grisby – then why kill Grisby? It didn't make sense. But it does now, with Bannister dead – and with her fingerprints on the gun!'

'Then Bannister didn't kill himself – *she* did it? You know for sure?'

He nodded, looking at her admiringly.

'She wanted it to look like suicide, like I said, and it would have, too, if we hadn't checked the prints. And that was just routine. The gun was found lying near his right hand, as though it had dropped when he fell.'

'And she killed *Grisby*?'

He was still rubbing her wrists, but it didn't seem to do much good.

'Sure,' he said. 'She was downtown that night, remember? She said it was to see a show. It was a show, all right, but not that kind. She was the most important one in it, though Grisby didn't know it. He thought that *he* was. He must have been surprised to see her, when he came up from the speedboat and found her waiting for him down on Wall Street. He must have been even more surprised when she pulled a gun on him – Bannister's gun – and shot him just like he would have been shot if you had done it sitting beside him in the car. Because the way I figure it, she knew all about the plan to kill Bannister, and just where you fitted in . . . they'd planned it all together; then they were to meet down in the South Seas. At least, that's what Grisby thought. They'd be free – you'd get the rap for it. But you nearly spoiled it by starting to run away. She had to hold you there, to make sure that you went through with your part. And in doing that she fell for you – she didn't want you to get the rap for it, after all. She's a very passionate woman, anyone can see that.

'But it wasn't for that reason that she killed Grisby – wanting to save you just made it easy for her to do. No, what I think is that she never did intend to run away with Grisby – she'd planned on killing him all the time. She'd have to, to get the hundred-thousand-dollar partnership insurance between Grisby and Bannister. And she'd have to get him *first*, so the money would go to Bannister. Then she'd have to get Bannister, so it would go to her. That wasn't the only reason she wanted to get him out of the way – she hated him. And then, in the end, there was another reason, too – she had to kill him to save you, or at least to try.

'Anyway, it all worked out fine. She got Grisby first, and then took the speedboat back to Bannister's beach – she was an expert, we found that out – and no one was the wiser. You confessed, as you were supposed to do, and the police just tried to make your story fit, that's all. The only one who might have told them the truth, probably, was Broome—'

'Broome! How?'

'I don't know how much Broome knew, of course, but there must have been a good reason for putting him out of the way. What probably happened was that he'd found out about the plot to kill Bannister, partly from your letter and partly from hearing her talk with Grisby. I could tell from Bannister's testimony at the trial that the real reason for Broome being at the house was to watch those two and find out all he could. But supposing we figure that Broome had found out about the plan and hadn't told Bannister at all, the way you thought, but had tried to blackmail her and get some of the money instead. He was louse enough. Or maybe he had just seen her walking up to the house after leaving the speedboat at the pier, and knew that she'd really got back at eleven-thirty or after and *could* have been down on Wall Street at the time of the murder. Incidentally, that's probably why she kept insisting that *you* were back at eleven – not just to help you, but to make it seem that *she* was back at that time. But about Broome – whether it was blackmail or what, if she knew he was a detective, she knew what he was there for, too – to watch Grisby and her and report to Bannister. She might not even have known what he had found out, but why take chances with him lying unconscious on the floor from your blow? The police and Bannister were out looking for you in the swamp – what could be easier than choke him with his tie as he lay there?'

Elsa began to show signs of life, but she didn't open her eyes and he kept on rubbing her wrists.

'And just as she tried to protect you – and herself – by setting the time she had seen you back at eleven – just that way she tried to handle Bannister's death. She figured that if she could make it look like he'd killed himself – and with the same gun used to kill Grisby – it not only would get him out of the way, but seem like a confession of his guilt. That way she hoped to save you and protect herself, too, if anyone had suspicions that she was the guilty one. And that way she'd get the money from Bannister's insurance, too – quite a piece of change, with the hundred thousand she'd get from the partnership insurance thrown in as a sort of bonus for good work.'

Elsa opened her eyes. She hadn't fainted at all.

'It isn't true,' she said. 'Any of it! Laurence, don't believe him – he's making the whole thing up!'

'Well, maybe I am guessing some,' said McCracken, 'but it doesn't matter. There's no getting around the fingerprints on the gun. You're on your way to the chair – right now!'

She stood up a little unsteadily.

'They'll never send me there. They acquitted the woman who shot her husband when he was raiding the icebox.'

McCracken shook his head.

'I suppose that's what gave you the idea. But there's only one man who might have saved you – the one who saved her – the one who took you from the chorus – Bannister! And you killed him – you thought he would be better off dead!'

She swept the red hair back off her forehead. Then she turned and looked at me, her lips twitching.

'I guess,' she said, 'that it doesn't matter now.'

I couldn't look at her. I bowed my head to hide the tears.

They got her for it. There wasn't anything anybody could do.

Galloway said that she had planned the whole thing from the start – tricked Grisby into going for Bannister, then killed him to make it seem that Bannister or I had done it; then killed Bannister, when he'd got the insurance money, to make it seem that he'd killed himself to get out of going to the chair for Grisby's murder.

He said that she was the cleverest, the most cold-blooded murderess that he had ever seen or heard of, and that if she had stayed on the stage she would have been a great actress, because she had fooled everyone right up to the end.

He had it all worked out, even about Broome and how he was trying to blackmail her 'in more ways than one.'

And he wound up by saying that *she*, not Bannister, was the one who would be better off dead.

The jury agreed.

I don't know. All I know is that I'm down here in Tahiti soaking up the sun . . .

Alone.